BOZAMBO'S REVENGE

BOZAMBO'S REVENGE

or

Colonialism Inside Out — a novel

By Bertène Juminer

Translated by Alexandra Bonfante Warren, with Preface
Introduction by Paul L. Thompson

Three Continents Press

First English Edition

This work was originally published in Paris by Présence Africaine in 1968 as *La Revanche de Bozambo.*

ISBN 0-914478-095 (Hardcover)
ISBN 0-914478-109 (Softcover)

Library of Congress Catolog Number: 75-42512

Front cover design by
Patty Zukerowski

4201 Cathedral Ave., N.W., Washington, D. C.

To Barbara.

Ou alors rien de tout cela n'arrivera, mais les gens, un matin, en ouvrant leurs persiennes, seront surpris par une espèce de sens affreux, lourdement posé sur les choses et qui aura l'air d'attendre.

SARTRE

Introduction

Bozambo's Revenge is Dr. Bertène Juminer's first work to be translated into English; consequently, a brief introduction to the author and his works is in order.

Dr. Bertène Juminer was born in Cayenne, the capital of French Guiana (Guyane), on the 6th of August 1927. His father was French Guyanese and his mother was from Guadaloupe. He attended grammar school and then the Lycée Carnot in Pointe-à-Pitre, Guadaloupe. After graduating from the Lycée Carnot, he studied medicine at the Université de Montpellier (France), receiving the "Doctorat d'Etat en Médecine" in 1953.

Dr. Juminer completed a considerable amount of specialized training in medicine and undertook assignments at a hospital in Saint-Laurent, Guyane (1956-1958), the "Institut Pasteur" in Tunis (1958-1966), the Medical School at Mesched, Iran (1966-1967), the Medical School of the Université de Dakar (1967-1973), and he is presently a Professor at the Medical School of the Université de Picardie (Amiens, France).

In addition to more than one hundred scientific publications, Dr. Juminer has written three novels: *Les Bâtards [The Bastards]*, 1961; *Au seuil d'un nouveau cri [At the Threshold of a New Cry]*, 1963; and *La Revanche de Bozambo [Bozambo's*

Revenge], 1968. He has also written a play, adapted from the latter novel, entitled "Archiduc sort de l'ombre," which won first prize from the French National Radio-Television Organization (ORTF) in 1970, and, just recently, the Cayenne based "Troupe Angéla Davis" production of the play received critical acclaim at the second annual "Festival Antilles-Guyane" at Cayenne (April, 1975); and finally, he has written a number of short stories, among which are "Le Résistant" and "La Pimentade."

With the exception of Léon-Gontran Damas (b. 1912), Juminer is the best known—and his works the most accessible—of the contemporary French Guyanese authors. Dr. Juminer has, for some time, been published by the Parisian publishing house, Présence Africaine, which has been a leader in presenting the works of black writers of the world—particularly those of Africa and the Caribbean area.

Guyane is a country which has, thus far, produced more poets than novelists. Damas has dominated the literature of the country and has been an author of pre-eminence in the whole area of black literature of French expression by virtue of his role as one of the founders of the *négritude* movement and his powerful poetry. A new generation of poets from French Guiana has now joined its voice to that of Damas in decrying injustice. Two of the most outstanding of these young poets are Serge Patient (*Le Mal du pays*) and Elie

Stephenson (*Une flêche pour le pays a l'encan*) who strive to express a reality and a sensibility which are specifically Guyanese. The struggle of these poets for such an identity is one which has led them to come to grips with their négritude as a means of combatting coerced assimilation into the ranks of the colonizer. However, the assumption of their *négritude* has not blinded them to their cultural mixture; consequently, a new identity has emerged which, through an amalgam of Africa and Europe, is, nevertheless, distinctly Guyanese.

A listing of novelists of French Guyanese origin would include, among others, the principal names of René Maran, René Jadfard and Dr. Bertène Juminer. Though it is not generally known, René Maran, who won the Prix Goncourt in 1921 for his novel *Batouala: véritable roman nègre,* was of French Guyanese parentage; therefore, French Guiana may, presumably, lay claim to him as one of her outstanding authors. The second major author, René Jadfard, was killed in an airplane crash in 1947. Jadfard was an adventuresome young man, as indicated by his best known novel, *Nuits de Cachiri,* which is based on his own experiences and is an absorbing account of the people and places encountered during an expedition up-river into the interior of Guyane. As René Jadfard explored the interior of the country, Juminer explores the psyche of its people—particularly the educated élite who are faced with the problem of cultural identity. In this respect,

Juminer's prose works show a stronger thematic affinity with the poets Damas, Patient and Stephenson.

Juminer's novels also reflect great concern for the political, economic, and social problems which faced his homeland. For many years, Guyane had little significance to the French government beyond that of a penal dumping ground and the country was left a backwater. In time it was discovered, however, that Guyane had tremendous mineral and other resources, the penal colony off shore was finally closed and, in the same year, Guyane became a "département d'outre mer" (overseas department) of France). New state and private investments began.

Most of the area's problems are a direct result of these four centuries of controlled neglect by France; consequently, Juminer and a number of other French Guyanese feel, to put it mildly, that their problems might very well be lessened if they were allowed to take remedial actions and to assume responsibility for their own country—in other words, they wish to use political power for the primary benefit of the Guyanese people. Their quest for solutions to their country's difficulties is part and parcel of their search for their own identity as a people and a land, as opposed to an appendage which has received the benign neglect of Paris.

Juminer's first novel *Les Bâtards* is to a great

extent autobiographical, being inspired by the author's two-year assignment (1956-1958) at a hospital in the town of Saint-Laurent in his native Guyane. During this period, Juminer was particularly struck by the almost total alienation of the educated, black élite from the great majority and their "local" culture—and by the quality, or the lack of it more precisely, of many of the French administrators. Dr. Juminer found that these individuals were nothing like the Frenchmen he had known and usually respected in France. Accordingly, his novel centers around the intertwined stories of the two main characters, Robert Chambord and Alain Cambier, as well as a subordinate, but very interesting character, Turenne Berjémi (an anagram of the author's name), all of whom are educated and to a high degree assimilated into French culture. They are, needless to say, aware of, and responsive to, their own culture which is first and foremost black. Their consequent intermediate position between these two cultures is indicated by the title *The Bastards* and their predicament as unusual beings emphasized by such an opprobrious term.

Au seuil d'un nouveau cri is an intriguing, didactic novel, which is skillfully structured into complementary parts, "Le Cri" and "L'Echo" dealing, respectively, with the black man's past and his present, vis-à-vis oppression. "Le Cri" recounts an epic myth in which slaves revolt against the tyranny of their masters and gain their freedom.

"L'Echo" is a contemporary portrait of the problems of the black man, with an exhortation to him to rise, as did his ancestors, to wrest freedom from the clutches of the oppressors.

In terms of mood, structure and style, *Bozambo's Revenge* is a radical departure from Dr. Juminer's two previous novels. Here the mood is satirical. An absurd world is created in which there is a reversal of roles between Europe and Africa (a reversal brought about ironically by Europe's continuing ability to maintain a genuine peaceful coexistence between its two dominant political ideologies: Capitalism and Communism). The situations brought about by the reversed role create a great deal of comic relief, for it is Juminer's contention that laughter—be it ever so bitter—is beneficial, for it offers the black man a temporary release from the ever present tension created by his oppression and, at the same time, it puts the oppressor into a perspective which blows away the cant and mystification of western colonial claims.

Structurally, *Bozambo's Revenge* lacks the complexities found in its two predecessors, and it is somewhat shorter. The tripartite structure of the *Les Bâtards* and the bipartite structure of *Au seuil d'un nouveau cri* were skillfully used to unite and reinforce several story lines and quite diverse personalities. In contrast, the simple narrative line of *Bozambo's Revenge,* mostly episodal, permits the author greater freedom for his polemical purposes and makes more telling his picture of the daily harshnesses of colonialism.

There can be little doubt that the most striking aspect of *Bozambo's Revenge* is the author's style, more specifically, his brilliant use of rhetorical devices and effects to structure a scenario of cultural reversal. As noted, the entire cultural oppressions of past and present being as much a matter of rhetoric as of physical power, Juminer's novel cleverly exposes the whole "show" by having the colonizers the "noble, civilizing" Baoulians from Africa, and the de-tribalized slum dwellers the "primitive" Franco-gauls of a sullen conquered province.

The French language, as does the English language, offers a number of examples of a more or less subconscious manifestation of the black equals bad and white equals good syndrome. Such innocent words as magic, list and market which, in and of themselves, do not appear to have any intrinsic color connotation, are made sinister by placing the adjective "black" before (or behind) them. From a black perspective, then, these words are preceded by the adjective "white" in order to take on a negative meaning. In the English language, a lie can be greatly minimized by calling it "white," and an illegal or immoral act may, through the grace of "whitewash" don the cloak of innocence. Juminer also reverses certain concepts, long cherished by some European cultures: "the white man's burden" becomes "the black man's burden," and the very popular *Tarzan* becomes *Zartan,* "the black hero who lives in the heart of the European jungle among the primitive tribes and savage animals."

Quite obviously, many expressions of cultural reversal, grounded as they are in the French language and culture, are not easily rendered into English, but there are a sufficient number of puns and cognates which permit word-games of similar thrust as to offer the English reader the serio-comical fantasies of the author with a high degree of integrity. The hundreds of uncanny reversals of roles: the historical pomposities, the clichés of prejudice, of fertility goddesses, of national monuments, of genocide and conquest, and the benumbing ferocities of the para-military colonial cadres ought to satisfy anyone needing a laugh or a snicker. But the rhetoric of *Bozambo's Revenge* goes beyond satire: it cauterizes away any possible belief in a system of cultural imperialism, no matter its "glorious" trappings.

Rhetoric, then, and the reversing mirrors of "reality" are the major devices of *Bozambo's Revenge*. Juminer goes as far as rhetoric can take him, but it is the "fantasy" of the work as a whole which lifts the reader up into the sad "sane" world of everybody's cruelty. Though the effective use of cultural parallels provides the joy of sour recognition and the reversals permit a "black" perspective, the novel is not a simple put-down of "whitey" or his arrogant past. Ultimately, it is a demonstration that racism—and economic and social oppression—are mad and lurid perversions of humanity—in themselves indefensible first and always.

Paul L. Thompson
Virginia State College

Translator's Preface

When we enter Bantouville with the immigrant natives, it is a travelogue narrator who pans over the visual surface of life in that city. The voice is one we are familiar with: the conventionally apolitical voice. But what it describes is an intensely political situation wherein one visually identifiable group is rigidly repressed by another. The narrator's language is slanted, however, and explicitly accepts the propriety of the situation, all the while it is maintaining an "objective" tone. Thus, for the purpose of the concept, the existential tension is established, and for the purpose of the plot, the political tension is as well. In *Bozambo's Revenge* they are identical. For Juminer, the idea of existentialism, when translated into the world of action, becomes politics. Action is, in fact, an acting upon.

Language, as the primary vehicle of communication between individuals and between groups of individuals must necessarily reflect this. It fulfills a two-fold function: it defines a group, enabling members of the group to recognize each other; and it defines a group with respect to other groups. There are several instances in the novel when it is a specifically linguistic act which brings about the radicalization (for Juminer this is identical with a coming-to-consciousness) of a character. When

Constance overhears her boss refer to his housekeeper as "boy," she becomes instantly aware of her political position with respect to Bozambo's class, and is moved to action.

One of the most characteristic and esthetically pleasing aspects of this novel is the diversity of voices: the language of Escartefigue's tract, the language of the newspapers, the "officialese" of the ruling group, and so on. The problem for a translator thus becomes that of rendering these voices into American English without Americanizing the characters and situations. Proper names have not been translated, and readers may amuse themselves with discovering some of the plays on words hidden therein. In cases where a pun could not be translated, I took the liberty of improvising one elsewhere when the opportunity presented itself. (For readers who "give up," we offer a few explanations at the rear of the book.)

Juminer's whimsy is expressed in the characters' sexual fantasies and (as noted in the introduction) in the inversion of white and black as loaded words in common usage, or in the substitution of an African context for a European one in idioms, proverbs, etc. He uses the French equivalents of "negro" and "black" interchangeably. At the time *Bozambo's Revenge* was written, "nègre" was viewed by blacks in France much the way "negro" is today in the United States–it represented the oppressor's word for the oppressed. When the political-power situation is inverted, as it is here, that connotation becomes meaningless. I believe this is an indirect hint on the author's part that we must realize the politics implicit in language, a concern shared by today's feminist movement, for example.

The key turning of the central plot relies upon a verbal ambiguity in the French original which does not exist in English. The French words for *grenade* and for *pomegranate* are the same. This is made fairly clear in our English text I believe, but I hope the reader will forgive any awkwardness which he may find we have exhibited in getting around this discrepancy.

The French *argot* presented a special problem. It originated among the "Rats" of Paris in the Twenties and Thirties as a language that the "Pigs" were meant not to understand. Most of the words Maggy and the Archduke use are the same as the underground used fifty years ago, or which can be read in Genêt, for example. American slang, on the other hand, is characterized by the fact that it evolves and changes rapidly and becomes dated for the originators by the time it is adopted by (usually) the middle class. Accordingly, I have tried for a standard American slang, with the sound of the urban black argot, this being the class which would correspond to the inhabitants of the Butte Mozamba.

The syntactical constructions are in general very close to those in the French text. My primary concern has been to render a text which the

American reader may study and (I hope) enjoy with a sense that its intentions, structure and language are reasonably close to that of the original, and have not been falsified.

Alexandra Bonfante Warren

Chapter One

1

If we may believe the account of certain historians, Bantouville is a kind of small paradise which African genius has created from a swamp by the banks of the Sekuana, a lazy and capricious river which the natives call the Seine. Her monuments, built by a noble and distant motherland, bear the great names of world history: from Queen Saramakaye of a thousand conquests, political and amorous, to the illustrious physicist Abou-Zuzuf, father of the theory of absolutivity. They arrive in the form of colored post-cards at even the most remote villages, from arid Provence to rainy Brittany.

Many of the back-country natives, reassured by the existence of a capital of such beauty, ultimately come to feel an unqualified pride in it, and gratitude towards the Providence which had them born in this part of Europe reached by African expansionism. They live in the secret hope of one day seeing this privileged city which is, after all, theirs. They dream of strolling gallantly down the great boulevards, visiting the famous monuments such as the Tour Abdoulaye, all metal and trapezoids, whose steel spire rises 150 spans into the air; or the splendid Baobabist Basilica built on Mozamba hill, the highest point of the city.

Sometimes the great day comes. Having bought a third-class ticket, and settled as best they can in an amazing chaos of baggages, food, and pestilential smells (to which are added the other dubious effluvia of bargain-basement travellers), they throw themselves into an adventure which, during an entire night, is a prelude to the labyrinthian dangers which make up their arrival and sojourn in Bantouville.

The clouds of cinders invading the compartments and turning you into a rheumy-eyed Negro in a twinkling, the spine-shattering jolts, the din which makes sleep impossible, the ticket-takers interruptions, all this is nothing compared to the reality of Bantouville.

After getting off the train, the white native is sifted through Customs and the Internal Migration Service. There are never any Blacks in the long waiting lines, since they are exempt from these formalities. While only a few migrants may be selected, apparently at random, for the baggage check (taking into consideration, among other factors, your expression, your clothes, and the Custom agent's mood), there is no chance of being overlooked at the identification control.

Policemen in blue or khaki bubus, according to the season, galooned and leather-strapped, assist the Migration Inspectors, and check each passport in an imposing file cabinet shoved against the wall. Their fingers seem to be perpetually pillaging the sliding shelves of the gaping cabinet which contains a directory of the local nonconformist fauna: politicians out of favor, underground labor organizers, saboteurs on the run, tax-payers who have disregarded a second notice, small-time smugglers, deserters and others on the white-list, each more ungrateful to the motherland than the last.

The white line is silent, waiting patiently at each window. Here and there on either side of the line, suitcases, baskets and bundles lay at the feet of their disillusioned owners, who are getting flustered as they muster the necessary papers: permit to circulate; certificate of Baobabist baptism; of employment; of good character; of non-contagion; and of residence in Bantouville. And so it goes in Baoulian Western Europe.

"Dagobert Martin!"

The man in question already has his hand out to take back his papers; he has not counted on the speed of the policemen at the files.

"Martin, huh?" the civil servant says again, "Any relation to the alderman?"

"What alderman?"

"Don't play dumb with me, everybody here knew Martin."

The inspector is correct in using the past tense. It has been a long time since that Martin was in Bantouville. He was sent to Baoulia for having dared to criticize administrative practices, a subversive activity if ever there was one. He would certainly have done better to have kept quiet in his white place as substitute teacher promoted to the rank of Sixth Deputy Mayor.

"Well, I don't know him!" replies the Sixth Deputy Mayor's namesake.

"What are you here for?"

"To work, what about it?"

"That's pretty vague. Got a job?"

"Well, I . . ."

"Okay, I get it. You'll get your passport back tomorrow at the Federal Building at ten o'clock."

Martin leaves the ranks with a hang-dog look. Perhaps he had thought that these misfortunes happened to other people. Or perhaps he hadn't thought anything at all. In any case, his number had been drawn from the Occupation's bag of tricks. There'll be quite a show at the Building tomorrow.

2

This is the first time that Anatole Dupont, young Provençal, is arriving in Bantouville. He has dodged Customs and after a bitter dispute with the Internal Migration inspector, has been able to justify his coming here, despite the family ties between himself and Edgar Dupont, his uncle, who seems to be well known to the Central Bureau of Information. Holding a Colonial School diploma, he would have preferred to go to Africa to drink at the fount of civilization so praised by his educators; but having no connections, he received only a half-scholarship for study at the local university. Any application to the Ministry of the Overseas Territories, seeking to attend one of the Home universities, is automatically rejected. So Anatole has resigned himself to coming to the Colonial capital and pursuing his studies here.

This very Amadou-Koumba train station where he has just disembarked, is quite instructive in itself. In a corner of the concourse the wall is torn open and covered with great patches of soot. Thick dust turns rainbow-colored in the rays of light falling obliquely from a large hole which an explosion has ripped in the glass roof. People come and go, affecting a feigned indifference toward this concrete wound, which is only the reflection of the one which festers in every conscience. Every indication, however, seems to point to an attempt on the part of the African militants, the Grayos, in response to Autocthonous propaganda.

A ground stewardess, an elegant African draped in a multicolored bubu, approaches Anatole with a smile and hands him a tourist brochure. She asks him about his impressions of the trip, and his plans for his stay. He answers with a string of lies which appear to satisfy her. The Administration has undertaken a grandscale offensive; in other words, there is nothing going on in Bantouville or throughout the rest of the Federation. The country is quiet and enjoys the unrestricted beneficence lavished by the motherland who can be proud of her achievement. Proof that all is for the best is the smile and the elegance with which the colonial capital receives her visitors.

Across from the station, huge slogans on the walls contradict each other with an obstinate and dry finality: "Free Escartefigue!" or "Down with imperialism!" express the demands of the Gallic Anticolonialist Movement, the ACM, whose Secretary General, the aforesaid Escartefigue is in jail.

"Up the Baoulian nation!" or "Down with secession!" are the militant slogans of the Pale Hand, the terrorist arm of the White Faces.

A cardboard suitcase at his feet, Anatole is looking through his pockets for the notebook on which he has written his uncle's address. He is overtaken by impatience and is going through contortions in the middle of the sidewalk which is swarming with people. He is shoved around, elbowed aside, tossed about. He is making a visible effort to stay calm. Suddenly, hit violently in the back, we see him thrown off balance by a white porter, panting and grimacing under his burden. He lets out a cry of protest which is immediately taken the wrong way by the other native.

"Hey! Who are you kidding? Think you're a big shot 'cause you talk like the bosses? Where do you think you are, anyway, Baoul-Bled?"

A circle of gawkers forms on the spot. Comments are running back and forth, noisily in favor of the porter, causing Anatole some discomfort. Hurt and embarrassed, he says nothing. The lower classes of Bantouville are not about to let a blackhorn like him give them the runaround. What could have posessed him to speak Baoulian to a native? In cases like this, even the African "bosses" speak Gallic.

To save face, Anatole starts to read the tourist brochure. This does nothing to increase his popularity, since a gesture like this can only create a humiliating gap between himself and those around him, who are, for the most part, illiterate. They turn away from him and a few offensive remarks reach his ears:

"Assimilated!"

"Baoulia-kisser!"

Seething with rage and confusion, he is careful not to look up. He learns the following from his reading:

> **During the barbarian, pre-Baobabist period, Bantouville, formerly a small village of pile-dwellings on the banks of the Sekuana, was called Paris and was the capital of a fairly advanced nation. Many Africans visited at that time and attempted to establish the healthy Negro ethos. But domestic troubles led to such anarchy throughout the entire Light Continent that the Baoulian Republic found herself forced, in the interest of peace and universal civilization, to impose her rule. Bantouville is today a**

> **magnificent city, numbering 300,000 inhabitants who live in harmony. The world-famous Champs-Baobabs, that splendid avenue laid at the beginning of the present century by African engineers, bears witness to the civilizing influence of our immortal Baoulia . . .**

Anatole slips the sheet into his notebook where he has just found the elusive address, stuffs both into a pocket of his bubu, and makes his way toward a raised traffic platform, occupied by an enormous Black policeman.

"Excuse me, Officer! Where is Rue Birago, please?"

The officer is pretending not to hear. Anatole, haunted by the recent squabble, has just expressed himself in Gallic. Unfortunately for him, his interlocutor is from the motherland. Realizing the inappropriateness of his action, Anatole repeats the question in Baoulian. Only then does the policeman condescend to lean over, to come down from his pedestal.

"Go straight along Avenue Modibo, until you get to the fourth intersection. That'll be Black-Hosts Square. Follow it around on the left. Straight ahead of you will be Boulevard Sékou. Take that and after about two hundred spans you'll run into Rue Birago. Got that?"

"Yes sir, Officer."

"Okay, and from now on, watch how you talk! So long!"

"Thank you. Thank you very much, and I'm sorry," says the downcast Gaul.

3

Suitcase in hand, Anatole is walking up Avenue Modibo. The main arteries of the capital bear the names of the great men of antiquity, writers, artists, and statesmen.

The sign on a tobacco shop reminds him to stock up on cigarettes since, although he didn't sleep a wink during the overnight train trip, he did smoke more than a pack of filter-tipped Baouliennes. On either side of the doorway, illustrated magazines and dailies hang from each other on metal clips. Some of the newspapers just in from Baoulia follow the hilarious adventures of the Galvinized Feet, Bobo Fikokin and other youth-cult figures.

Head up, Anatole comes out of the tobacco shop. An enormous inscription scribbled awkwardly on the wall in front of him hits him head on: "Peace in Corsica!" It is a condemnation of the tragedy which has been going on for years in the Overseas Territory of the Maghrebin Republic.

The Corsican fellagha are carrying on a fierce struggle for national independence despite the intervention of a regular army of Pacification, and, aided by members of a native auxiliary contingent, they are striking a serious blow to African imperialism. Sardinia and Sicily, who have only recently gained their independence, support the rebels, and the Ministers of the Provisional Government of the Corsican Republic (the P.G.C.R.) have taken asylum in these sister countries.

This fence is scribbled upon by the Pale Hand, no doubt about it. "One Maghreb, from Tamanrasset to Bastia!" "Lose Corsica and you lose the Maghreb!" Anything goes in this peculiar war: sabotage, liquidation of personnel, hijacking. Five of the principal Corsican leaders are rotting in Maghrebin prisons following their capture in a plane over the Mediterranean.

One could, for that matter, wonder what Europe did to bring onto herself the implacable African domination. Decadence? Congenital weakness? Historians and archeologists agree that at one time, Europe had reached a certain stage of social organization, but opinions differ when it comes to explaining its importance and nature.

The question is absurd for those who admit no civilization or culture save the Black. A civilized Europe? You must be joking! She was nothing but a wasteland, or nearly; a place of anarchy and bandits, until establishment of the colonial outposts.

Even here, the myriad archeological remains in Bantouville could not persuade these scholars of the reality of a European Antiquity which reached its apogee around 40 Before Great Baobab and was the work of pink-skinned Africans who settled in the area. Where did these Africans come from? We do not know with certainty, but no one disputes that they existed, the unusual coloration of the epidermis being, from all the evidence, an adaptation to the climate.

The Europe of that time appears to have checkmated herself, to have become rigid and weak from being unable to choose between two ways of life, both, however, conceptualized by her. While one aimed at national development by initiative in the private sector, the other postulated well-being as a result of the resources being in common ownership. When peaceful coexistence between these two systems became impossible, there rapidly followed the death-throes and, finally, the death of the white continent.

A few learned men, officially regarded as dreamers or anarchists, have held other, rather startling beliefs. White and non-Baobabist, Ancient Europe had lived in prosperity until its people came to pursue a fatal course which led to imperialist expansion, that lethal poison which as we know, strikes a brutal blow to the motherland.

This heroic attempt at demythification, deemed scandalous by Baoulian colonialism, categorically refutes the thesis of a pink-skinned Negro, referring to authentic documents where it can be formally verified that the great men of ancient Europe had white skin and straight hair. Their vassals, on the other hand, were almost all dark-skinned or black, and were labelled niggers, spooks, coons, shines and niakhés, generally accompanied by an abusive qualifier. Living in a patriarchal society, these Europeans of old practiced a monotheistic religion which represented God in the image of a man. This evidence should, according to the author (to whom we can only wish a speedy release from prison), suffice to invalidate once and for all the racist theories of Black scholars . . .

The violent beep of a horn causes Anatole to jump, interrupting his reverie and forcing him back onto the sidewalk. With a screech of tires, a car has just come to a stop, and the middle-class African behind the wheel makes an obvious gesture of tapping his temple with his index.

"Why don't you watch where you're going, paleface?"

Anatole does not reply. There is nothing to reply. Besides, the car has already taken off. Heavily, he begins moving, and mutters through his teeth: "Son of a colonialist!"

4

Around Black-Hosts Square, political propaganda has given way to huge billboards advertising Bora Belkoukoune's (a.k.a. B.B.) latest film in wide-screen and Africolor. She is a very attractive

African, whose legend has reached a planetary dimension. Anatole stops to contemplate her. A generous brush has accentuated the flashing smile, given an added touch to the perfection of the bust, sculpted the curve at the small of the back, raised the posterior contours of the famous star, superbly molded by a clinging minibubu.

He knows that he has never imagined a more desirable woman, and, like so many other native fans, he will not miss her in this superproduction in Africolor. During his childhood, he has seen, for the most part, films tracing the colonization of *ouolove* America. Lost in an impressive luxuriance of sand and forest, African pioneers, champions of civilization, sacrifice their lives to bring the continent out of the darkness. Aside from these edifying spectacles, adolescent Anatole thrilled at the exploits of Zartan, the black hero who lived in the heart of the European brush, in daily contact with primitive tribes and wild animals.

Today, this kind of film disturbs him. There are always the colonial dances: bourrées, sardanes and other farandoles: whites cavorting to the sound of tambourines, instruments which have neither the majesty nor the depth of the tomtom.

Here is Boulevard Sékou. Anatole turns on to it pensively. The mere prospect of finding himself in a line of Bantouvillians marking time in front of a box office window, of finding himself forced to elbow his way through, of being told off by some impertinent person, unnerves him. He asks himself if he will go see B.B. after all.

He has gone scarcely a few spans before a startling scene presents itself, although what he is discovering is fairly commonplace in Bantouville. A native beggar is trying to soften the hearts of passersby by whining an old song imported from overseas. By the wretch's outfit one may guess that he took part in a military campaign at one time, or that he forced the generosity of a native infantry-man. Shod in old down-at-heel military boots, his legs encased in frayed puttees, he is lost within an old khaki bubu, while a shock of grizzled hair peeps in washed out tufts from under a chechia. There he is, settled in against the wall, directly on the sidewalk. His eyes are maliciously febrile, one leg is crossed over the other in a paradoxically aristocratic pose. He is conscientiously attempting to sing: "I want to see my Baoulia again, where I first saw the light of day!"

At the corner of the boulevard and Rue Birago there stands a cafe from which emanate the strains of a juke-box, sending forth a best selling folk tune: a javanaise solidly arranged with bala-fons, ritis, koras and tomtoms. When did Anatole come in here? Here he is standing at the bar under the forceful eye of the President of the Republic of Baoulia whose color portrait hangs above the well-stocked shelves. He is in full regalia: across his bubu the massive braid of the Order of the Immortal Baobab. Despite the threat of obesity following his recent operation (in which he cheerfully sacrificed a banana to save the regime), President Mango Zekodene cuts his usual fine figure. About one span tall, massive, his abdominal muscles visibly held in in front of the camera, he looks his best and does not fail to impress.

Elsewhere, on the other walls and in the room, the power of the African which seems to pour from the presidential gaze is reflected everywhere. There are painted panoramas of Baoul-Bled, the city of lights, and artistic, military, and legislative capital as well; there are ebony and ivory figurines and masks, reproductions of the works of ancient and modern masters, obviously arranged with care to strike the imagination. Bursts of customers' voices discuss current events, such as the struggle of the whites of *ouolove* America to obtain integration in the schools hitherto reserved for Blacks. A few, more civilized, Europeans, wearing African dress and speaking the same but with a strong toubab accent (they rasp their r's instead of eliding them properly), reinforce the conviction that, in these places, the African is indeed in conquered lands.

Signs on the walls stipulate that correct dress is required. This means nothing more than that black foot must be shown at the door; that is, bubu, Baoulian and, on gaining admittance, a bow or short meditation before the presidential portrait. Anatole has fulfilled these requirements, yet he does not dare take a seat at a table. We should mention that they are all taken by Blacks in the company of emancipated Gallic women, who are particularly arrogant.

Most of the colonial administrators leave their legitimate wives in the motherland, frightening them with the rigor of the colonial climate. As soon as they arrive in Europe they set themselves up with a string of native mistresses. Polygamy remains a firmly established institution throughout the entire Baoulian empire and is without a doubt the only one enthusiastically embraced by everyone, regardless of faction.

Barely a cubit away, two administrators are regaling each other, unconcerned by Anatole's proximity. At each rejoinder they churn the air with copper-colored hands and the panels of their bubus spread like the wings of giant butterflies. Carried away by the discussion, they begin little by little to drift, forcing Anatole to bend backwards and to read on an individual level a metaphor of the *rapport de force* between two continents. Europe keeps quiet and backs off before Africa. There is not, nor could there be, a dialogue between them and this is even in the best interests of the people whom history has condemned to silence. Everything which is happening in here and outside cannot but reflect the difficult confrontation between the African spirit and the backwardness of the rest of the planet, and testify to the Black man's burden.

"Can't wait to get back to the Big Apple!" says one of them. "This rotten European climate is killing me. I'm planning a good sun and health cure in Timbuktu over the holidays."

"I'm going to the shore. Already rented a place in Dabou, on the Opal Coast."

"I don't think I'll come back here. Three years in the colonies working like a honky is plenty."

"Then there's the problem of the kids' education. They certainly can't continue their studies in Bantouville. . . !

"Of course not! A little more iced lagmi?"

And on that note, already a little pale from drinking, they clink their glasses.

Anatole leaves without ordering anything. He feels ashamed. He has travelled almost five hundred kilospans to come to Bantouville for an education, and he finds out that those who are serious about it go back to Africa where even the climate is better.

The reverberation of the street catches him up as he walks, head down, carrying with him his silence and his bewilderment. In the cafe there echoes an enormous peal of laughter, resounding with a terrible sardonic quality: a Negro laugh. He will never know if this laughter was directed at him, but he suffers nonetheless an atrocious internal wound.

His suitcase in hand—what reflex allowed him to avoid forgetting it at the bar?—he walks slowly down the street. The house he seeks is still far, very far, in the direction of the outlying districts; it does not even have a number. On the piece of paper lost in his pocket there is written only: Dupont, extension of Rue Birago. Extension? That places the area: certainly a half-abandoned nauseating neighborhood, where poor whites are crowded into disgusting promiscuity; the native quarter; the ghetto.

5

Farther back, behind Anatole, steel-tipped boots are hitting the sidewalk rhythmically and the sound is all the more distinct since the street is practically deserted. He does not deign to turn, but just keeps his head up and looks straight ahead. But for the entire length of this slightly winding street, leading to the outskirts of town, nothing catches up to him and nothing recedes. He is alone, his burden in hand, ideas in his head, followed by this mechanical squeak, whose echo strikes him with the regularity of a clock. He remembers what he saw in the Amadou-Koumba station concourse: the waiting lines; the peace-of-faction police here, there, everywhere; those fierce inspectors from whom he has just escaped. Suddenly he is disturbed. That's a patrol coming up back there. He is carrying a suitcase. These days, any person with blancoid features found so equipped at more than three hundred spans from a train station is considered suspect. There ensues a systematic, meticulous, hassling search accompanied by an interrogation which ends with the opening of a criminal dossier. This always takes several hours, at the end of which there is little chance that the questionee will be blackwashed, exculpated.

It is well-known that nationalist groups do not shrink from the most underhanded methods: distributing leaflets, writing subversive graffiti on public buildings, mutilating statues of the African benefactors to humanity. This says a lot about the proverbial ingratitude of the natives. They're all the same, just liars and layabouts. Try to tell the good ones from the bad ones, especially when anticolonialist propaganda has reached their childlike consciousness! What's more, they do not even trust each other and without the Baoulians it would be chaos.

"Kiddo, there are two dangers to watch out for in Bantouville: the whites—our brothers!—and drafts." Thus spake Anatole's father. And now this patrol of native infantry in their puttees and field-service blue bubus. He would have liked to have continued walking calmly, to have appeared unconcerned, and to have let them pass without even appearing to notice the six white soldiers, armed with cocomacaques* and led by a black

*Billy-clubs

sergeant. Instead, instinctively, he starts to hug the wall and his step quickens. At the same time, the cadence of boots sounds like the rumble of a locomotive. He has to gain distance if he doesn't want them to catch up. He makes a quick turn at the next corner and runs as fast as his legs will carry him.

When the patrol arrives at the intersection where Anatole has vanished, they realize that the native with the suitcase is now no more than a desperate fugitive. This is all it takes to convince them that it is a question of a subversive element preparing to strike a blow at the domestic and foreign security of the State. At a brutal whistle from the sergeant, the infantrymen take off after Anatole whose bubu is fluttering absurdly in the wind.

If you do not have the good fortune to be Black, it is not advisable to run through the streets of Bantouville. This situation, already serious in itself, becomes complicated when the fugitive has to wander at random, running the risk of going in circles, encountering a guard at a public building, getting busted by plain-clothes cops, or seeing loom before one an urubu-wagon*.

Feeling himself pursued, Anatole abandons his suitcase onto the sidewalk. Although he is greatly disturbed at leaving a valuable posession,

---

*White Maria

which could, moreover, help to identify him, he is discovering the surprising power which his position of outlaw suddenly confers upon him. The same expression of bewilderment and fear crosses the face of each person who looks up or turns to see him coming. Blacks alone, women especially, are frightened (the Pale Hand displays heroism only when backed up by the forces of so-called order). Anatole, meanwhile, is pitting all his courage against his desire to become invisible, and his raging stride becomes a sidling glissade up to the corner of a building before taking off again, nervous and halting.

A few overly made-up and perfumed Negresses, holding children by the hand, or accompanied by white boys, laden with baskets and the little students' book bags, shriek with terror. When the patrol arrives on the scene they pull themselves together, pointing in Anatole's direction, where he is stumbling into yet another corner.

"That way! He went that way!" The boys, who are already lucky to get room, board and drink at their bosses' expense, become as inconspicuous as possible. In their hearts they wish the fugitive success, but they are also relieved at not being in his place. As a matter of fact, it doesn't matter if one has anything to explain or excuse or not, since it is obvious that any white without an alibi will do.

Soon the whistles cease blowing; the chase ceases as well: the soldiers have just fallen over their commanding officer who has stopped abruptly to examine the abandoned suitcase.

Anatole doesn't want to know what is going on behind him. He doubles his efforts and starts to wander through a quarter which becomes more and more densely populated. And here he is, out of breath, coming out onto the Place Léon G. Soumaké. Some men, their chechias pulled down over their eyes, whom Anatole keeps jostling, do not appear to have clear consciences. They freeze, pale and haggard. Electrified, they contemplate Anatole for an instant, since he is already on his way without so much as an excuse me. Then, they understand without another moment's hesitation: "Beat it, you guys! The Man is after a brother!" one of them, who seems to have some experience of this kind of native-hunt, shouts. There is a sudden rush toward improvised shelter, a real panic.

A few ladies of the night, paralyzed with surprise or unable to run in their tight clothes, suddenly take on the rôle of maids on an errand. Others, who have jumped parole from the vice squad, hike their bubus up to mid-thigh and scamper away like kantchulis*.

Some illicit merchants, called bana-bana toubabs, who make a living slipping vials of wine or

---

*Rats

pornographic photographs of the local prostitutes onto the white market, disappear into the cafes run by fences. A few white-is-beautiful songwriters and artists who have come to this picturesque area at the foot of Mozamba hill to find inspiration, find themselves suddenly alone, blonde or brown hair dishevelled, brows wrinkled, brush or pen suspended in mid-air, among the thiep*—sellers who are trapped with their carts against the sidewalk; while the strains of a javanaise still filters out from a few pubs.

Place Léon G. Soumaké, despite the good-natured air which its central fountain, the bistros surrounding it and its under-shirted athletes lifting hundred-kilo weights lend it, is one of the rare sections of Bantouville where the Man does not venture, whether in plain clothes or in uniform. On the whole, the individual elements of the local fauna know each other well and while some rivalry may pit them against each other, they observe an unspoken truce and show a common front to intruders, without, however, ceasing to fear each other. Police detectives, policemen and their minions on the police payroll are immediately exposed, tracked down, sometimes liquidated between two hallways with the suddenness of black lightening. One does not enter this world without the safe-conduct of unconventionality, and one leaves only via white-maria or ambulance (which

*Fish-and-rice

often amounts to the same thing, as the urubu-wagons have been known to pull up at the morgue).

So, all things considered, Anatole is fortunate to have made an entrance which earns him both respect and attention. When he sees everyone scatter and no attempt to stop *him* or report him to the police, he feels that henceforth, this is his world. True, those who fled from him were primarily concerned with their own well-being, but there is a kind of sympathy directed towards him which emanates from the rout. So it is here that he must stop to rest, especially since he is overtaken by fatigue and since to continue his course along the Boulevard Sékou (where, by happenstance, he has found himself once again) would only expose him to another unfortunate encounter.

6

In the Bistrot de la Butte, he is greeted by a questioning and solemn silence; this native Areopagus is evidently a newcomer. A few pseudo-customers, partially concealed behind open newspapers (which they would be hard-pressed to decipher, since most of them are illiterate) and others, not daring to reach for their hastily-served glasses, observe him furtively, convinced that this man who has arrived in their midst is a V.I.P. Anatole parks himself, panting and disoriented, at a table where a red-headed woman is seated. He takes no notice of her. No doubt about it, they think, this guy is a heavy. This must be his neighbor's opinion as well. She smiles at him now with a kind of deferential gratitude.

"Would you like to order, sir?" asks the owner who has appeared instantly.

"Hey! Why're you talking to me in Baoulian? Where do you think you are, Baoul-Bled?"

This last is spoken in a loud and distinct voice, with a 360° glance around, as if to call all present to witness, and, at the same time, to edify them. The result is immediate and conclusive. Anatole is a patriot and a reprobate, and therefore true-pink. The porter's lesson has not been in vain. A simple sound of boots, and a few whistle blasts have added the finishing touches.

"Bring me a shot of wine!" he goes on calmly in Gallic, pulling a short clay pipe from his pocket. "Then I'll want a paper!"

The owner, who was disappearing, turns, acquiesces with a bow, revealing his hopeless baldness, and, in that posture, backs away until he backs his coccyx into the cashier's desk. He will not have to execute the order since the young woman has promptly plunged her hand into her bag and come up with *Baoulie-Soir* which she offers to Anatole.

An enormous headline on the front page: "The terrible drama of Babacar Grobonda Square." It tells the sinister story of a substantial robbery of some African administrators, compounded by murder. Needless to say, the white boy is under suspicion. Furthermore, he has disappeared. It was certainly the best thing for him to do, since innocent or guilty, he would have had a few uncomfortable moments with the Bantouville police who are almost exclusively made up of Blacks.

On the second page, another headline catches Anatole's eye: "Two hundred thousand Whites marched on far away Samoryville yesterday!" Then, in bold-face italics, "We will go as far as we have to, non-violently, to obtain equal rights with Blacks," asserts their leader.

In the four centuries since Africans first set foot in America, the misfortunes of the white race have been multiplying. First there was the slave trade, where Whites were sold by their own people to break their backs under the whip in mean agricultural tasks for ten generations. Then came the abolition of slavery, not without a struggle that shook the entire continent, from the foulbephone United Provinces of America to the Tierra del Hielo in *ouolove* America. Paradoxically enough for anyone acquainted with the Negro's innate inhumanity, a few men and women of the black race joined this struggle whose goal was to throw off the yoke of African imperialism. Koumba Couli-Cagou did this with his thrilling book *Uncle Jules' Hovel*; then Vivi Oumarou in the Caribbean carried on after the white hero Laclôture died of thirst and heat, deported to the farthest confines of the arid Sudanese savannah, despite which his victorious country became the first white republic of the New World.

At the present time, there exists in the U.P.A. an atrocious segregation at the expense of the white minority. To each race its own neighborhoods, its own public establishments, its own vehicles within the public transportation system. Side by side but never together, except in the case of a general mobilization, and even then! Even soldiers killed in action are rigorously separated. If segregation implied equality, it would be at least a lesser evil. In fact, however, the standard of living, the societal possibilities, and the political rights of Whites are, for all practical purposes, reduced to nil. They say that in front of certain public places in the U.P.A., reserved for the Black privileged classes, one can see the sign "No dogs or Whites". It is sadly straightforward, albeit rather unfair to the dogs, who in many cases are permitted where Whites are not. So true is this, that some recent anti-segregation demonstrations have been quelled by police dogs–Kabyle shepherds specifically–who had no reservations about tearing cornered white trash to shreds while a powerful blast of water pinned them to the ground or hurled them against a wall. And after all this, there are still Whites who say that the more people they come to know, the more they love their dogs.

As for the American Whites, they still cling to nonviolence, they still volunteer to be loaded onto trucks, hymns on their lips, to be taken off to prison. It appears to be a mania with this race to sing while it's being martyred. To Anatole, this attitude is insane. Any struggle for equality with another is absurd. One does not use reason in fighting to share the future of the privileged, one overthrows them. Since inequality is at the very foundation of their society, there can be no possibility of an equitable distribution. One might as well suggest a full tube of Congonal for each of them, to be taken at bed-time.

Here in Europe, the essential struggle is not for integration, but rather for liberation, that is, the departure of the Occupier. As the Corsican fellagha proclaim: We must choose between the supply-wagon and the hearse.

The deep roots of the racism perpetrated by Negro power around the world must be sought in the basic structure of African society. The African has never ceased to try to free himself from the matriarchal yoke and all his expansionist tendencies bear the mark of this obsession. Thus, the two advanced bastions of African civilization overseas, Baoulian Western Europe and *ouolove* America, are at the whim of black emigrants trying to escape the matriarchal eye and practicing a rigorous compensatory exploitation of the subjugated white tribes. In Europe this takes the form of colonialism, in America, racial segregation. The white woman exerts an erotic fascination over all these racist Negroes, lynchers and White-baiters. Clearly there would be no racial problem in the United Provinces of America if the white minority were made up of only women.

It may seem paradoxical, but in the motherland, the African woman is rarely blancophobic. Her preëminence is assured—there is practically no competition. On the contrary, since she is permitted everything, she carries refinement to the point of disdaining black men in favor of the Whites who come to drink at the source of *Baoulophonia.*

As for the Creole woman of America, she is certainly as racist, if not more so, as the African. It is a sign of great realism on her part because she knows that the white man must be kept down if she is to maintain her supremacy. This acts as an excellent outlet for black males, subject since time immemorial to an oppressive vulvar imperialism.

"Real bastards, those Blacks!"

The woman has just spoken. Anatole starts, then considers her thoughtfully.

"Bunch of sadists," she continues, "I've seen in the newsreels how they treat us: trained dogs, cocomacaques, fire-hoses. . . they beat on women, old people, children singing in their best Sunday clothes, with nice clean gloves, going to church. . . "

"Us Whites, we're fools! As long as we keep

singing hymns we don't deserve any better than to get thrown in the can for blocking traffic."

"Don't say these things. They hurt me as much as they do you. We saw you come in a minute ago."

"So? Did I sing? Did I wait to get arrested?"

"What are you going to do now?"

"Why do you want to know? Who are you, anyway? I don't know you."

"What does it matter as long as we're on the same side?"

Chapter Two

1

Along with the residences of the colonial administrators, the administration buildings are the most beautiful and comfortable edifices in Bantouville.

The spacious, well-lit offices of the Department of Territorial Security are situated on the sixth floor of the Federal Building and overlook the foliage of the plaintains on Avenue Tonton-Makoute. It is similar to a cockpit, with its ceaselessly humming multiple machinery, the dials with their oscillating needles and eternally blinking signal lights. The room designated for the director is the geometric locus of the vital connections of the city, a brain where all nerve impulses converge and are deciphered. Nothing is missing. Not even the portrait of the President of the Republic nor, in vases on either side of the double-pedestal desk, a plastic baobab on one side, and on the other, the Baoulian flag, hanging down its pole.

This functional space, a sort of privileged cell, enjoys an autonomous regulation, independent of nature's cycle. There are only two seasons in colonized Europe: wintering and summering, since the African authorities have decided that, in man's image, the climate must accede to the plan for general and controlled integration. The folk notions of spring, summer, autumn and winter have been banished from the calendar and only have meaning in the heart of the rural populations of the back-country which are still under the influence of certain traditional chiefs.

Moreover, the factories of the State only manufacture two varieties of bubu: one in a light cotton cloth, for summering; and one in waterproof wool, with long sleeves, and sometimes African cuffs, for wintering. Thus the sartorial habits of the citizenry continuously recall Nature to her duties.

Wintering began officially on the fifteenth of Bananuary*, that is, the previous day, and there is still a suffocating heat. No matter! All the employees of the Federal Building have put on their wool bubus, and if the heat is not on, it is because of a recent sabotage which damaged the boiler.

A man of tall and strong build, of Ashanti extraction, Inspector-General Bozambo has a large, extremely mobile face, albeit a bit heavy, wherein shine very expressive black eyes. A part in the middle, which seems to have been done with a razor, divides his kinky hair, giving him an opera-bouffe appearance. One would be mistaken in going by that. He is an intelligent, shrewd man, experienced in colonial affairs, not for nothing the man in charge of territorial security for the O.B.E. The renewed outbreak of native restlessness in the

---

*September, to the Gauls

last few weeks despite official, but behind-the-scenes, support of the Pale Hand, is a serious annoyance to him. Hundreds of suspects are questioned daily, arrested after curfew, interrogated in vain; their dossiers pile up in the police files and accomplish nothing except to lengthen the notorious white-list. Apart from a few overt agitators such as Escartefigue, who calls himself the Secretary-General of the A.C.M., almost all have had to be released. Not for lack of proof—should the necessity arise, you can always invent some—but in the hope that tailed by agents, they might lead to the leaders. But even in this the results have been disappointing. For the subversive graffiti increase and multiply, the mutilation of statues continues, poison cabbage leaves are still in circulation, hidden under bubus, carrying orders which are more and more disturbing.

As is his wont, the Inspector-General grabs the telephone receiver at the first vibrations of the ring.

"Hello. Bozambo here! I'm listening."

"Hi, Boz! This is Mamadou Sar. I've got something for you."

Colonel Sar, who graduated as a major from Bouaké Colonial School, is military commander of the post. He's an old chum of the chief of the D.T.S., they count their friendship in lustres. They went to grade school together, then to Behanzin-the-Great High School, and stayed together until it was time to choose a career. Their paths crossed again in Bantouville, by the whim of colonial chance.

"What about?"

"This afternoon, one of my patrols chased down a suspicious native. Looks interesting. A civilian, so he's your baby . . . "

"Arrested?"

"Still running . . . "

"Baobab almighty! It's the same old story!"

"But he did drop a suitcase en route. Shall I read you the report?"

"I'd rather you send me a copy."

"You'll get it, old man! I just wanted to give you the scoop as soon as possible."

"Go ahead."

The colonel begins to read the report which has made its way through the hierarchy to him:

"Today, Lunal*, Bananuary 16, a native infantry patrol, Sergeant Ibrahim Makoko of the 117th regiment of the Colonial Infantry (Europe Sector 3) in command, attempted to question a native carrying a suitcase. The latter, subsequently found to be in contravention of regulations . . . "

"What jargon!" the colonel interrupts himself to say.

---

*Monday, September 16. In Baoulian, the days of the week are: Lunal, Marsal, Mercural, Jupital, Venusal, Saturnal and Solal.

"Congratulations!" retorts the Chief of Security, your men are champs at it!"

Mamadou Sar, used to this sarcasm, takes up his reading without missing a beat, especially since he has a distinct aversion for those N.C.O.'s who juggle gibberish:

"The latter, subsequently found to be in contravention of regulations in effect concerning the circulation of physical persons, escaped, instead of obeying the customary summons. In light of this fact, and judging a second summons to be unnecessary and superfluous . . .". The colonel interrupts himself again: "This verbiage is exhausting, let me skip a few lines and get to the important part:

"Just as the subject was about to be apprehended, he dropped his suitcase and the Infantrymen were thrown ribs to ground, colliding with the receptacle . . ."

"Thrown ribs to ground?"

"Oh, hell! They fell down!"

"Oh, quite! Very clear! What's this receptacle?"

"I guess it's the suitcase . . . Anyway, you'll find out for yourself. I'll sum up the rest fast, because it's getting late, and I've been invited to dinner."

"Colonel Sar dines in oil?"

"Knock it off! It's been said, and besides, you're extending it beyond its maximal verbal potentiality! So, our man took advantage of the confusion and disappeared. Inside the suitcase they found a peculiar package addressed to a certain Edgar Dupont, Extension of Rue Birago. The bomb squad was notified. 'Bye, Boz. Good luck!"

No sooner has he hung up in his turn than Bozambo calls in his secretary, a pleasant blonde Bantouvillian, believed to be his mistress. Panting from the sprint, she stands before her boss, whose long fingers rest casually on his desk.

"Constance, go find me this man Dupont in the files right now. He keeps turning up like a goddamned bad Baoul. Get me his dossier as soon as possible."

"Yes, sir."

"Also, call my house and tell my boy he can go. With this job ahead of me, I certainly won't make it home for dinner." Constance, poured into the latest word in bubus, has vanished, swiveling hips, spike heels and all.

The case is disturbing, thinks Bozambo. It is the first time that suitcases have been used for explosives. It lends itself to the many transportation networks which exist throughout the city. Usually, these "receptacles," as the Sergeant would say, are stuffed with clandestinely printed leaflets, or with paper money for the C.L.F. (Corsican Liberation Front), from the anticolonialist activists.

"If the toubabs are really starting to act

up . . . !" sighs Bozambo pensively, "there'll be a lot of nights counting okapis."

Constance is still upset following a telephonic squabble with Frederick, the boss' servant. She was furious when she left the chief's office at being forced to learn once again how Baoulians spoke of whites, and she felt a solidarity with the poor bugger who had so off-handedly been described in her presence by the pejorative term *boy*. She had picked up the receiver determined to display a special warmth. "Hello, Frederick! This is Inspector General Bozambo's secretary . . ."

And he had replied patronizingly, "*Monsieur* Frederick, if you don't mind! We didn't grow up together, you know!" He had even allowed himself to speak Baoulian.

The elevator stops in front of the door to the security files which occupy the basement. A well-devised system permits one in a matter of minutes to collect information on anyone who has been stopped and questioned even once. Countless Bantouvillians, therefore, unbeknownst to themselves, lead a subterranean life under cover of napthalene.

It is here that Constance has to pick up the trail of the aforesaid Edgar Dupont. What pleasure she would have had doing the same job at the expense of that animal, Frederick! But instead, she must contribute to hamstringing a few natives who dare to defy colonialism. Ever since Escartefigue's arrest, she has hated her boss, him and the rest. As if by some sort of telepathy, some activists had sought her out at the very moment she was wondering how to join their struggle. A spectacular coup was wanted–sabotage within the Federal Building itself. And that was how she had come recently to throw a plastic "sandwich" into the boiler of the heating plant.

An old, one-legged asthmatic guard sits on a stool, his wooden leg out in front of him. He has the good fortune, as a disabled vet on pension, to have a lifetime position, and spends most of his time serenely smoking his pipe and remembering the high points of the last campaign he was in from beginning to end as native infantry against the South African barbarians.

"Don't trouble yourself!" says Constance, who does not trust him.

She enters the cool room and turns on the light. Here she is, in front of a file going through the letter "D." In the process, she reads, one after the other, out loud, the names of her "contra-vening" compatriots: D'Eugolles, Dupanloup, Dupont. That's it! Now to look for the Baobabist names. She has gone through one hundred and seventy-three cards before getting to Edgar. It's amazing how many Duponts there are in Bantouville. Finally, she finds the one she's looking for: Edgar Dupont, forty-two years old, skilled worker (at what, good Baobab?), married, eight children, living on the extension of Rue Birago; distinguishing characteristics: agitator, registered member of the Baoulian Radical Party, affiliated with the B.C.–B.F.T.W. (Bantouvillian Chapter of the Baoulian Federation of Temporary Workers). N° 197 263.

The guard, keys in hand, accompanies Constance to the cold and obscure storeroom where the dossiers are kept. He walks in front of her without a word, puffing like a bellows, striking the tiled floor heavily with his peg leg. In this semi-obscurity, filled with the smell of pipe-tobacco and floor-wax, his wheezy thumping evokes the atmosphere of a misty marshalling yard. The storeroom is on a slightly lower level, which one arrives at by going down a few stairs.

The rhythm of the guard's wooden leg slows down, his hoarse breathing speeds up. The keys click against the lock, the door creaks on its hinges behind Constance who has left her companion outside.

She has found the right dossier immediately: it is a voluminous pile of papers, in a heavy cardboard jacket, well-tied with string. Something must be done for this brave father of a large family who, with such a weighty judicial past, cannot hope to escape the terrible mustachios (inspectors specialised in the repression of subversive activities). So she quickly unties the packet, takes out a handful of documents, leaves them on the shelf, then hies herself back to the sixth floor.

2

The only charge against Edgar Dupont, so far, is that of inciting workers to strike, which is against the law and punishable by hard labor for life. The guilty party, however, benefited from extenuating circumstances by reason of his family situation. All the other indictments rest only on circumstantial evidence. Judicial use of these would have been a grave tactical and political error which Bozambo has been careful not to make. Convinced that he is now on a promising track, he plans to go over the various pieces in the dossier carefully while waiting for the inspectors who have gone to look for Dupont. One of Escartefigue's pamphlets "What is Baoulian colonialism?" attracts his attention. Bozambo takes the opportunity to look it over, for although he signed the order for its ban and seizure, he has never read it. And he finds himself caught up by the dialectic of the anticolonialist leader, expressed as follows:

The cult of talent represents one of the most flagrant contradictions of the so-called evolved peoples, and it is in the area of received ideas that these contradictions attain an atrocious power of harm. In mass cultures, everything takes place as if individuals as such had ceased to exist. The nation's symbols quickly force themselves onto the individual, creating for each person a standardized coat-of-arms wherein the slightest episodes of ancestral heroism are emblazoned. Even the proletariat of the motherlands, their necks under the foot of a well-fed bourgeoisie, cling to the same values as this middle-class so as to help crush the entirety of the colonized peoples (from the beginning defined as the dark to the colonial power's light—in an old manichean tradition). Identifying with the pioneers, in fur moccassins, scarves, sweaters, and leather helmets, the masses take pride in empire and vaunt themselves of their extensive domains. The masses come to the conclusion that, all in all, international life is nothing but an unrewarding relationship between a handful of their sort exhausting themselves in order to give, and a multitude of ingrates who reach out to take without so much as a smile.

This is the reasoning of the eternally exploited class which adopts a general superiority solidifying into a simple opposition of colors: the colonized White is a lazy savage; monogamous and therefore immoral; Christian and therefore ungodly; without a history and therefore without culture. On the one hand, the black elect, born to conquer; on the other hand, the white damned, stricken with a congenital complex of colonializability. Thus, any corrupted culture will ultimately move into a jingoistic era which tolls its death-knell while claiming an apogee.

The colony confers letters patent of nobility and everyone seeks to be considered a member of the upper class. All colonized peoples find themselves willy-nilly in the same bag: those who dream of a more breathable air have no choice but to struggle for liberation. At the heart of the colonialized world there emerge two kinds of nationalists: those who seek to justify themselves, and all the others. The former guard the realm of the spirit and, obstinately scrutinizing the past, wear themselves out seeking positive qualities to oppose those of the occupier. Obsessed with cultural rehabilitation, these archivists charge forward, pen in hand; set off here and there a few tempests in an inkwell and die in their beds of old age. The others, too pure for these hypocritical games, take their reality to heart and engage in a struggle which tempers the newly awakened consciousness of their brethren, and, when these nationalists come to write history, they write it with their blood. There is only one tangible meeting point between these two types: exile or prison (which is but a kind of internal exile).

For centuries now, Africa has dominated the world and Europe has constantly acted as her foil. Whites must not be ashamed of these truths, nor use them as a cause for guilt as the imperialists would have us do. The true exploiter knows neither repentance nor pity, and her allies, whether of color or origin, never disown her. It is therefore a waste of time to try to appeal to the feelings of the powerful. It is true that they were so intent on depriving Europe of her memory that she is tempted to gather her past and brandish it like a weapon. Certain Whites are forever salting old wounds such as the trade to which their race was subjected by black slavers. This unpacking of old gewgaws makes no sense, even if Kolombu—that old African pirate—in discovering America by accident did give the signal for a vast genocide. In fact, one has to agree: time is on the side of the enslaved peoples of Europe and ouolove *America. The West is stirring, and even though it continues to appear to be what Africa wants it to be (a giant pie of which each black power received its share, prorated according to political and military might), the signers of the Bobo-Dioulasso treaty were mistaken in their belief that that was the end of it. Because carving up a nation has never killed its soul.*

In certain milieus it could be asked why I am not writing this statement in Baoulian, the official language imposed by the Occupier. It is tempting, as a matter of fact, to argue that formulating a demand in the very language of the masters would be the most effective means of establishing a dialogue with them, of pricking their conscience. To this I reply that I do not recognize any conscience on their part, good or bad. Therefore, I have nothing to say to them, since everything has been expressed, or perpetrated along the only lines that have ever characterized our relations with them: that might is right. But one does not remain the mightiest forever.

Our role, as Whites dominated by Africa, by her weapons, her wicked economic doctrines, her religion and her culture, is to regroup, to set off and to carry to its conclusion, our struggle for national liberation. It is to my brothers in misery that I speak. I want to reach them all: those who have lost themselves in the African culture to the point of forgetting our own (those are, it certainly seems, the intellectuals); those who have attended only elementary school or no school at all, because they were forced at an early age to go work in the factories (since imperialism has built an industrial and severely vegetarian civilization on the backs of our race); even those who accept the uniform of the native Gallic infantry and put down our revolts; and, finally those who have not only converted, but become priests of the Baobabist religion, that religion whose cynically avowed aim is to eradicate our ancestral faith. Everyone must join us, sooner or later, to take an active part in the struggle because no matter how severe the mutilation, the deep roots survive. Our language is one of these roots and the occupiers can tell us as often as they want that it's just an undeveloped tongue, but we will not give it up. And so it is in Gallic that I wish to speak.

There is another flagrant contradication in the colonial system that must be exposed; in that colonial system which is crushing us even as it hypocritically pretends to be fulfilling a mission for our own good. They tell us: "Your very primitive dialect must disappear. Learn our beautiful African language which is spoken by an entire continent, the most powerful on the face of the earth." So we learn the beautiful African language! And our masters snicker when they hear us, they put us down in public, they ridicule our 'honky-talk'.

"By the holy name of Baobab," says Bozambo to himself, "the toubab's got a point! Let's see what else he has to say."

Even our names, Pierre, Paul, Jean, amuse them. Since these names aren't on the Baobabist calendar, they are only fit for colonized people such as us. This constant pressure, this overt desire to convince us of our destitution sometimes bears fruit: some of us decide to take the leap, to approach the occupier. They begin by naming their children Mamadou, Babacar or Koumba; or, even if they live in the most remote village, they abandon the suit for a bubu. But since, as often as not, their inadequate education does not allow them to master the colonizer's language (except to sing imposed hymns, or to recite some banal imported poem) it is in our own language that they congratulate each other or call to each other. This expresses a deep-rooted will to resist the colonizer despite themselves.

No one in my family has ever worn a bubu or borne an African name. My name is George Edouard Ferdinand Escartefigue and none can claim to be more Gallic than I. If, like all my schoolmates, I learned that my ancestors were called Baoulians, that they had black skin, kinky hair and wore their enemies' testicles around their necks, I never really believed it. I am white; where I come from, we have been white from father to son. I have no Baoulian ancestor. So it is in Gallic that I wish to speak.

I intend, by doing this, to deprive the imperialist of a simplistic argument that he uses against us when it serves him to do so, that is, our so-called ingratitude. From time immemorial, whenever a colonized person has criticized the imposition of an alien culture, and extolled the rehabilitation of white values, the black imperialist has stood and fought with petty diversions. This was the case, about thirty years ago, when some of our university students, exiled to Baoul-Bled, smack in the middle of colonialist Africa, launched the white-is-beautiful movement. White art was taking over the world at about that time. The famous White Review *was drawing the cream of Baoul-Bled which was dancing to the beat of the java and crowding the galleries to admire our expressionist paintings. From that moment everyone knew that something was happening: the colonial world was raising its head, and the bold ones, those who dared to hold their heads high, were the very people, from Copenhagen to Gibraltar, who were subject to an abominable racial segregation. From the rutabaga fields of New Zambia, white music was retracing its steps back to the source, detouring through imperialist Africa and forcing it to be affected.*

"That's a bit much. Have to check this out," murmurs Bozambo, getting up for a kola nut which he chews nervously, and continues reading.

There were other, in-house, brave ones, in the highest circles of black culture, who had resolved to lay the foundations for our cultural demands, preliminary to our political demands. It was a good tactic because the Black man was overwhelming us, denying us the existence of any culture antecedent to his intervention. We Whites were nothing but savages with prelogical mentalities, just barely capable of absorbing whatever intellectual nourishment they saw fit to laboriously concede us. It was at that time that a few students sang out that white is beautiful, challenging, once and for all, the exclusive input of the masters, and postulating our participation in the development of world culture. In his Record of a Return to the Land of My Ancestors, *Lamine Zamba cried out pertinently: 'My whiteness is neither a bombax nor a baobab.'*

"Nicely put!" judges Bozambo. "Too bad it's unfounded."

Unfortunately, this splendid refusal, despite being expressed in Baoulian, at first touched only a small number of Africans, a minority which favored decolonization; the rest kept silent or feigned indifference to this admirable work which handled their own language with a rare perfection. Despite the difficult vocabulary, this achievement evoked considerable enthusiasm at all levels of the colonized world, even in the children attending rural schools.

Reactionary Africans still ignore this manifesto. Conversely, they seize any opportunity to denounce our so-called contradictions (the best proof that cultural assimilation is a blessing is the fact that our demand is circulated in Baoulian), and our ingratitude (is this the thanks that Africa gets for patiently educating and instructing us?). Therefore it is necessary for me to speak in Gallic.

But I will not only speak. I want to shout, to take up Lamine Zamba's threat: 'And I will hurl my great white cry so chillingly that the foundations of the world will tremble.' And my ambition is to go further, to bring all the colonized peoples to discover the necessity of going further, collectively, and organized.

Until now we have never had a true leader. Those who spoke for us were not willing to pay the price that our struggle demands. Our mission of liberation must follow a double path: dialectic and action, or it will not be at all; because it is not enough to discover some miraculous keys, even with great clamor; one must also be prepared to use them.

Seen as the only means of liberation, clinging to the phrase white is beautiful, and wringing it dry, dialectic is doomed to failure. Not only does it not set off any profound echo in the masses, it even reassures the imperialist who goes so far as to enter into the game, so as to bury the essence of our demands in his own cultural mystique. And so it is that any conscious colonized person sees the necessity of going beyond a slogan into political action: that is to say that he is ready to accept all the consequences. It is only from that moment that communication with the masses is established and becomes a threat to the occupier.

"Well, old man," sighs Bozambo, "It's a good thing you're in the can!"

A dominated people always comes to recognize those who, by their example, show them where the path to dignity lies. In these conditions, any leader who is persecuted must be considered authentic, since his punishment proves him to be a real threat to the colonial system. Conversely, any dialectician who is tolerated must be considered suspect by his own people.

I know how much annoyance these truths will arouse in African circles, and I can already imagine certain reactionaries shrugging their shoulders and exclaiming: 'Try to tan a white, and you just get bleached!' With all due respect I hope we insubordinate toubabs get them very bleached. Insubordinate we will obstinately remain, even if our baoulization were to culminate in our accession to the comforts of African civilization.

For a long time now we have seen through the colonial ruse which consists in corrupting us, settling us in insignificance, throwing us (crouched with a bone in our teeth) their scraps. Nobody is unaware, least of all those who give it out, that this largesse is merely a golden reef against which our belligerence is meant to shatter. Then imperialism can laugh up its bubu, spit on its hands and step up the pressure.

It is a fact that the Africans laugh at us a lot, and that the Negro laugh, with its falsely warm trills, represents a formidable factor of demoralization for those who are its butt. It becomes necessary to desensitize oneself to it. Once having neutralized its effects, nothing would be more useful than to turn it against those who use it. This is no small matter. Many colonized people have tried to do so—but in vain. Tired of the effort, they end up laughing at themselves, humiliating themselves, and, by so doing, painting a sad picture of our mentality. And so it is that the movement to collect that laughter and throw it back in the oppressor's face is pitifully aborted and becomes self-destructive.

Paradoxically, the capital of white power is still today Baoul-Bled. It was in that city that the "great white cry" was uttered by the university students. The role of the educated person within our struggle is quite clear, but this struggle is running a fatal risk if it aims solely at a cultural objective. The promoters of white power were so convinced of this that they all became involved in politics. But we must specify the nature of this involvement. If to act politically consists of obtaining an appointment from an essentially colonialist party, in order to intrigue for a parliamentary mandate, so that once the electoral success is assured, the appointee may go sit in the Baoulian National Assembly and ratify there the very laws which enslave us, then we declare that treason has been committed . . .

A light begins to wink in front of the Inspector General who learns from this that his men are in the elevator. Having no more time to finish the Dupont file, he closes it, then lights a cigarette in order to recover a certain nonchalance before interrogating the accused.

3

When the few short knocks echoed on the door, Edgar Dupont thought that it was his nephew who had finally arrived. So he hurried to answer, without bothering to change his suit and put on the bubu thrown on a chair. He shares this habit, this sartorial double identity, with many natives: traditional costume at home, bubu in the city. He had nearly leaped from his chair, a sudden fever seemed to have overtaken him at the thought of hearing news of his family. He unlocked the door, pulled it open, and found himself face to face with two black cops who did not appear to be lost.

"Are you called Edgar Dupont?"

"Yes. What do you want?"

"We'll ask the questions! Come with us and hurry up!"

The inspector who had spoken was already on his way out, thumb thrown behind him to indicate that Dupont was to do the same. His younger colleague (a rookie for sure), surprised by this cold determination, was standing with his mouth open, his thick lower lip drooping unnaturally, dragging with it cheeks, nostrils and eyelids. Thus deformed his face seemed to be reflected from the mirror of an aging coquette. He continued to look around the single dirty room, at the odds and ends, at the piles of old, disembowelled mattresses, rickety tables and heterogeneous crockery. Ten people lived in this, and it was a miracle that there wasn't more noise or confusion.

Heaped in a corner, a barely-pubescent young girl, certainly not yet circumcized, held a sleeping baby on her lap. You couldn't see her very clearly, but you could imagine in her a precocious maturity born from poverty and responsibility. The six boys, between the ages of these two children, were somewhere in the area, playing in the garbage of the municipal dump. The mother wasn't yet back from work.

"Who are you?" asked Dupont again.

". . . Until you're spoken to! Come on, let's go!"

He didn't even have time to give his daughter last minute instructions. What for? It was the fourteenth time he'd been pinched. At his house, everyone made allowances for this. When he didn't come home, no one got frightened. His wife would simply say: "Edgar got popped again," and go about her business, thinking that at least it was one less mouth to feed.

During the entire trip to the Federal Building the inspectors didn't say a word. They smoked, or chewed kola nuts which they pulled by the fistful from their pockets. As for Dupont, since he didn't know what they wanted, he was asking himself a thousand questions. Putting a few weeks of freedom to good use, he had engaged in several subversive activities since his last incarceration. The most serious of these activities was to set up Escartefigue's escape. Poor guy! If the plan was uncovered and the network discovered, he was done for. So he decided not to think about it, but the white bile continued to rise in him, there in the White Maria, despite himself.

At the moment, he is not very pleasant to look at as the inspectors have somewhat rearranged his face. His lip is torn, he has a white eye, he is subjected as well to the painful insistence of a spotlight aimed at him. Droplets of sweat slide and jump nervously down his blow-swollen cheeks.

And now one of the inspectors returns to the attack after a long, refreshing drink of water.

"So you claim you know nothing about the statue gang? Then how is it that all the statues within a hundred-span radius of your house were mutilated?"

"I don't know what you're talking about."

"Okay, then, let me refresh your memory, you little bastard. At the beginning of wintering, two statues in your neighborhood were desecrated: Patrice La Rumba's and Dudu Glissant's. In both cases, the same type of mutilation occurred. Now that's a signature!"

"I don't know anything about it."

Two sounds occur simultaneously: that of a brutal backhanded slap across Dupont's face, and the inspector's unpleasant, derisive laugh. The head of the accused wobbles for an instant in the luminous beam, and a trickle of blood appears at the corner of his mouth. Dupont is well aware that this interview is merely a preliminary to the real nitty-gritty: for, earlier, at the time of his last interrogation, the case of the sabotaged statues had led to a vast round-up.

"You son of a rhinoceros! You didn't know that La Rumba's beard and Dudu Glissant's mustache were smashed? Or that Dudu is still cracked and that your pal, that so-called journalist Renaudot (whom we'll be busting soon) claims it gets the prize for the best number of the year . . . Last week, a stone's throw from your house, other outrages were perpetrated on Tintin K. Taillé's statue. The great orator's pipe was broken."

All these statues have had to be hidden in wooden casings until they can be restored.

"I was in jail when that happened."

"Bloody liar! You were released three weeks ago!"

"I'm talking about the beard and the mustache."

Dupont realizes his poor choice of words only after another slap. These inspectors have been nicknamed mustachios, and they don't like it at all. They themselves avoid using the word and always say bacchantes. As it is they considered the attack on Dudu as a personal affront. To come along and throw this intolerable word in their face, within the Federal Building no less, appears as reckless provocation.

"If you're gong to act like an asshole, you'll get shafted all right. Now let's talk about the bank-note and stamp gang."

This was the fourteenth time the matter of the bank-notes has come up. Here are the facts: in order to express their discontent, or sometimes just to ridicule the occupier, the natives put out the eyes of the great men whose pictures appear on the paper money. The five-thousand B.C.E. baoul* notes—commonly called marshals—are the most popular. They bear the likeness of Field-Marshal Amoakonte-Deumo, that great empire-builder to whom Baoulia owes its colonial power. Then, the thousand-baoul bills, on which is printed the profile of the Military Witch Doctor, Keskonfé-Dessu who conquered Blood-on-the-Brain, the dreaded scourge of the first pioneers in Europe. It is rather significant that Baoulia joined these two illustrious men on its paper money. Wasn't it Amoakonte-Deumo, that famous maker of opportune aphorisms (whose motto was: "Show the assegai so you won't have to use it") who said to the Minister of Defense: "Send me a witch doctor and I can send you home a batallion!"?

Of course Dupont has on occasion put out the Witch Doctor's eye, or blinded the Field-Marshal; but not as often as he would have liked since his scanty and rare emoluments did not allow him to handle big bills. Luckier than he are the "boys," entrusted with fairly large sums to shop for their masters; they pull over for a moment en route, unfold the bill, punch it once or twice with a pin, and that's that. As for the stamps, Dupont really doesn't know anything about that.

---

*Baoulian Colonial Europe. One B.C.E. baoul is worth two mother-country baouls.

"Come on, admit you sabotage the bread!"

"I've never even handled a *marshal*," says he piteously.

"Watch it, Edgar! Insult Baoulian currency and I'll belt you again!"

He corrects himself: "I have never owned a five-thousand baoul bill. I said that before. Right here. Thirteen times."

"What about the stamps?"

"What stamps?"

"Look at that!"

Somebody shoves an envelope addressed to Bozambo himself into Dupont's face. The picture of the great star Bora Belkoukoune which appears on the stamp has been hideously defaced. The young woman, whose smile shows every tooth, sports an enormous mustache which turns up into zebu horns. Such a sacrilege must have irritated the chief of security and his men terribly. All the more so since the letter itself bore a disgusting message in Gallic, "Down with colonialism!" and signed, *A Patriot.*

Dupont looks at the stamp, repressing a bitter urge to laugh, and retorts: "I don't know how to read."

"I don't give a good goddamn whether you can or not!" the inspector thunders. "I'm asking you to look at this stamp that your dirty colored brothers did a number on!"*

Bora Belkoukoune, with her toothpaste smile and her bacchantes is truly grotesque.

"I don't know this gentleman," says Dupont.

The inspector leaps to his feet, grimacing with fury, raises his arms to the heavens in a characteristically Baoulian gesture, trembles with rage and utters inarticulate noises.

And now he is striding away shouting: "What a bottle-gourd! Who stuck me with this coconut?" A hair's breadth from a nervous breakdown, he exits through a door which he slams behind him.

It is but a brief respite. The other inspector then takes Dupont in hand and begins to speak to him in a honeyed, almost friendly voice, to create a new atmosphere.

"So tell me, Edgar, where does your wife work?"

"At the post-office."

"How about that! Quite a coincidence, don't you think?"

"You know very well my wife had nothing to do with it. All she does is keep house."

"Maybe so. But you could have, for instance,

---

*The inspector is expressing himself correctly. The great physicist Abou-Zouzouf brilliantly demonstrated that since black is the absence of color, it follows that the colored man is the white.

given her the idea, or given her the instructions to pass on to another employee. Get the picture?"

Dupont sees only one picture: if his wife is arrested as well, what will happen to his eight children?

"Hey, you wouldn't bust her?"

"I wouldn't, huh?"

The door opens noisily and the other inspector reappears, even angrier than before. Arms akimbo, he plants himself in front of Dupont and, nostrils quivering, looks him over with disdain. Dupont suspects that there is news, he is on guard. He is well acquainted with the tactics of angry mustachios: they pretend to go do something else, then all of a sudden you get a punch in the head, and it ain't no love tap.

"You can go," barks the inspector. "Come on, get the hell out of here!"

Dupont doesn't wait to be told again. He knows the way very well, so don't bother to show him out. He leaps to the door without waiting for his change.

4

All things considered, Bozambo doesn't really buy this explosives story. He knows his natives, from the real derelicts, the vagrants of Place Léon-G.-Soumaké (which abounds with pickpockets, enigmatic pimps, down and out ex-athletes, syphilitic dope peddlers, and penniless bards of white power), up to the politicking trade unionist fauna among whom are a few pencil-pushers on the edge of the middle-class, and gradually losing virulence, until, with one or two bundles of five-thousand baouls on their tongue they become silent altogether. One could do a study on that, he reflects, especially on the social itinerary of those colonized persons who have become legends within the regime in their lifetime. And all the Escartefigues in the world could never deny that the real colonialists are those autochthonous social climbers who exploit their white brothers and sisters to join allegiance with the Blacks, an allegiance which, furthermore, they do not sell cheaply. Thus the ruling Africans suffer a parasitism more scandalous than any form of colonial exploitation, since they get nothing in exchange.

All of them, from the humblest to the most powerful, are nothing but a bunch of smartasses and cowards. Their only goal is to take the Africans' place, or at least come and keep them company, and share with them what they consider privileges. As far as that goes, only the Whites enjoy the so-called privileges since the poor black administrators have to suffer the evils of the colonial climate, of being far from home, of the administrative hierarchy, of being separated from his family.

The experts of the bomb squad, under Commander Adiami, see sabotage everywhere.

Bozambo has his doubts. Even here, they raised an extraordinary hypothesis: that the explosion could have been caused by explosive jelly. This is becoming an obsession! As if it were even thinkable that a native would risk his life inside the Federal Building for this kind of mission, inconceivable in itself. It is not in the nature of the toubabs to resort to violence: everyone knows they're just overgrown children. How could they be heroic?

Instead, Bozambo believes that the package addressed to Dupont contains tracts or confused pamphlets along the lines of Escartefigue's. Moreover, that's the ambition of all natives: having once received the generous African culture they think of nothing but pretty speeches and pretty political or other writing, so they can puff themselves up with having mastered vocabulary, grammar, syntax and semantics. Knights of the Ink-Well, all of them.

It is a fact that Dupont, a skilled worker and doubtless under-educated, couldn't be a pen-pusher; on the other hand, if the nationalists had really decided to raise hell they would surely not have entrusted their explosives to him, a man eternally under suspicion, and known as the white wolf. At most, he could function as a kind of barker for the amusement of the peanut gallery, and even then . . . !

Bozambo starts. What if Dupont were merely a diversion? What if there really were a network of desperate men ready to put the city to fire and sword? No matter how much you say the toubabs aren't mature enough, you can't deny the possibility. He remembers that in Corsica, the nationalist leaders were overruled by the militant radicals and forced to change tactics. What if the same were true in Bantouville?

Out loud he says, "That's all speculation! I let myself get caught up in Escartefigue's jabberwocky."

He realizes that in expecting to lose sleep over it he has even overrated the matter. There is no Dupont affair. And he chuckles for a while, as if to put the whole thing out of his mind.

Suddenly he gets the urge for a woman. Nothing like it to make you forget your troubles. In a little while he'll go home with his secretary Constance, to his magnificent residence on the Left Bank. A light, cold dinner, a kola nut or two for energy, a few glasses of palm wine, some jazz, that music of the Negro renaissance, and then to bed. And if he does stay awake, it won't be on account of Dupont, but to beat his monkey, dip the nigger, to work until dawn on the famous triangle, in search of the square of the hypotenuse.

"As for heating, it'll be central *and* explosive! Eh, my dear Adiami?" he snickers, mocking the Commander of the Bomb Squad.

As if on cue, the phone rings and Adiami is on the other end of the wire.

"How about that!"

"How about what?"

"I was just thinking about you, bro'. Just now!"

His bro' Adiami would certainly not be happy to know what Bozambo was thinking about him. But he is rarely interested in such things, and it's really too bad.

"I should hope you're thinking about me! The Dupont affair is serious. My experts found grenades in that piece of luggage that was under suspicion."

"What! Grenades?"

"To tell you the truth, I don't know anything about it. Just that they were found. Your move, Boz. 'Bye!"

And he hangs up. No doubt about it, Adiami isn't very curious, or else he's pretending not to be. He is discretion personified, especially when—as is the case at the moment—it is closing time, and he has a romantic assignation.

This nonchalant way he has of cutting off a conversation, in other words, of washing his hands of it, irritates Bozambo. The bomb squad experts announce that they have discovered grenades, in some way prophesying a disaster, then without further ceremony dump the whole thing in someone else's lap. Every time. They arrive, ceremonious and pontificating, expressing themselves in some tight-assed jargon (one asks oneself if even they know what they're talking about), decide that there's plastic jelly here, grenades there; if you disagree with them, you're the world's biggest fool. If you agree with them, you don't do much better, because in any case they disappear immediately, hopelessly vain and scornful.

If that were the worst Adiami did! Publicity-seeking to the point of obsession, he always sets things up so that it is he who receives all the credit and all the praise. Barely thirty, he is already a colonial commander, posted in Bantouville and official prognostication points to a stunning promotion. Just last week, in the middle of a reception, the Secretary General of the Federal Government, a descendant of the glorious Field-Marshal Amoakonte-Deumo, whose name he bears, grasped Adiami's hand to read his palm, and announced before a sympathetic audience, to nobody in particular: "Commander, in less than ten years you'll have bombax leaves on your sleeve!" What a mockery it would be if Adiami were to become a general before the age of forty!

Bozambo can visualize this show-off clearly, leaning back in his chair, his galooned chechia at a rakish angle, confiding to his friends after a good shot of palm wine: "The territorial guys? Don't make me laugh! Without my infantry patrols and my flare-shooters, they'd be in a lot of trouble!"

Bozambo is fuming, "He's a sop, a wormy sop!"

He doesn't even remember buzzing for his

secretary just before the phone call, nor does he remember the excellent plans he had quiveringly made.

"Here I am, boss," says Constance, suddenly appearing before him.

"What do you want?"

"But you rang for me . . . "

"It was a misunderstanding. Get back to your typewriter."

After dismissing her, he feels his rage growing and leaps to his feet to go have a couple of words with that animal, Dupont, still stewing in the hands of the mustachios. That bastard! We'll show him grenades! Bozambo's part is oscillating, swept now here, now there by his constant frowning; his eyes, usually laughing and mobile, are glaring with annoyance. He strides nervously into the hall. Here he runs into one of the inspectors who, stricken, is staggering around, apparently suffering from a case of nerves similar to his own.

"That guy is completely dumb, chief! We can't get a thing out of him!"

"Son of a manioc! You're the one that's nothing but an old rotten gourd! No wonder the Archduke is still on the loose!"

Since Escartefigue's imprisonment, the Archduke has become the prime mover of anticolonialist subversion. He gives orders, signs his names to tracts, maintains a veritable legend of invulnerability and messianism around him; his name alone galvanizes the crowds, and all the nationalist leaders, like Escartefigue, who are presently in the can, appeal to him as their authority. As of this moment he has miraculously escaped capture, to the point, that, except for Bozambo, most of the police force consider him a kind of ghost that walks. But Bozambo won't give up. The Archduke exists and must be captured, or subversive activity will only increase and multiply.

"Dupont's just a poor son of a hippo, chief. His stupidity is doing us in."

Bozambo feels his legs fail under him. You'd think the whole world was mad, or that Dupont, suddenly transformed into a tough nut is playing with these idiots.

"Shut up! You're the one who's doing me in, fire-eater!"

The inspector pales. Fire-eater, the supreme insult, expresses such contempt that it often leads to tragedy, awakening as it does the memory of an ancient twist of fate in Baoulian history: the wars of religion between the Apostolic Baobabists and the fire-worshippers who had, at one time, hoped to reform the faith. In the end, the fire was never able to consume the Baobab who, on the contrary, smothered it in its shadow and strength. Today, to be called a fire-eater ranks you even lower than the frog-eating natives.

"You shouldn't call me that, chief. It's not fair."

"So you haven't understood that this toubab is taking you for a ride?" retorts Bozambo, dodging this serious incident with his subordinate, whose fist is clutching the gun in his hip pocket.

"Maybe not . . . But I'm not a fire-eater!"

"Okay, let's forget it. Where are we in this interrogation?"

"The statue, paper money and stamp gang."

"But that's ancient history!"

The inspector's contained fury increases; he has a fierce impulse to smash his fist into the chief's face, to cram his insults and unfairness down his throat. He starts to hate him, to wish him nothing but frustration until such time as he is called back to the mother country for disciplinary action for incompetence. It's not surprising, he thinks, that all Europe, baouliphone and ouolophone, is seething with revolt. Empires are lost through just this kind of leader.

"Did you talk to him about the suitcase?" Bozambo continues.

"Not yet, chief."

"Very good." The inspector, who was expecting to be bullied some more, is now at a loss. "I had to start over from scratch with the accused," he says to excuse himself.

"Very good. We have to release him. Come and see me afterwards. Go on."

Bozambo has turned on his heels, leaving a confused underling behind him. He wants to get his hands on the Archduke at long last, and show everyone that he was right to believe in his existence. He has no picture of him, not even a fingerprint, but he has imagined him so often that he is sure that the original will correspond to his mental picture. He will spend all his time on it if need be, but he must succeed in catching him and turn to his advantage this singular contest which pits them against each other. He has a plan now. He will let Dupont go, not even allude to the explosives and put a permanent special detail to follow him.

Chapter Three

1

The day dawns timidly at the foot of Mozamba hill. It is the hour when truck farmers, street sweepers, knife-and-scissor grinders take over the street which the dubious nightwalkers have abandoned: the cruising pimps, thirsty catiapes* and mokobites*, fearless tafars**, querulous mibunes** and makumests**, greasy ones and other pickers-up-of-soap*** who wear the fluttering Tantusian bubus. It is also that uncertain hour when the dreams of those who exercise small, honest trades take shape, while a truce is declared between the different shareholders of those local enterprises specializing in the exploitation of "les horizontales."

A puddle of light dances over the water jug and, reflecting across the dimness, comes up against Anatole's eyelids and wakes him up. He reaches his hand out for his companion who had offered to let him share her bed. But the young woman is already awake and busy in the little kitchen adjoining the bedroom. Maternal as all get

---

*Prostitutes

**Homosexuals

***A ribald saying of the O.B.E. says: "See who bends over to pick up the soap in a men's shower."

out, she cradled Anatole on her bosom all night long, but he was careful to vaccinate himself robustly against an Oedipal complex, and to reinforce the vaccination with booster injections. In short, he has truly socked it to her, going so far as to make certain demands, the better to play his role as the bad boy he is believed to be.

And yet, no one could be more mundane than he and, despite a touch of the intellectual conferred by his certificate from a colonial junior high school (although on the Butte Mozamba such a diploma is not that unusual), he sees this new dawn through the eyes of a provencal country boy. He knows that he has been very lucky in escaping the patrol, and to find this young lady about whom he knows nothing and who treats him like a lord. What would have become of him in this city that he is just beginning to discover, with its traps, its dangers and its dreams, what would have become of him if not for her? . . .

Back in his village, human contacts reflect a stable epidermal hierarchy: there are the good colonizers and the good Whites. The two racial communities live in harmony, side by side, periodically mingling on official occasions such as national commemoration days, the birthday of the president of the Baoulian Republic and holidays of the Baobabist calendar.

The Negros impose laws that they alone may break. The Whites accept the subjection to what they see as a Purgatory: they send their children to school or catechism, pay taxes, give up their young men to the conscription officers. And then, having paid their dues, they meet with each other in the large marketplace, their souls at rest, to talk interminably and pass the time until curfew. In other words, happiness reigns down there.

The administrative officer has placed his power under a double aegis: the smile that beckons and lulls; and the force that intimidates and brings one down to earth. He has a colloquial quality and doesn't hesitate on certain summering afternoons, to join the local notables in a game of bowls under the plane trees. Needless to say, he always wins, but this kind of initiative goes straight to the indigenous heart. He likes to quote statistics to support his arguments, because production is the primary goal of modern Baoulia. Less waste! The white man must fight against his congenital laziness in order to lessen the burden of the Black man who has been committed for centuries to the immense effort of universal civilization. The native population, feeling itself so well understood, is jubilant and enthusiastic. Volunteers for portaging come running from every direction, recruited by squadrons of armed native infantry, recruited in their turn by Baoulian N.C.O.'s.

The Military Witch Doctor plays the progressive. He has always spoken out against portaging. He comes to the villages on his regular sanitary rounds or in emergencies. In theory he no longer goes about on manback since he was allocated a mule, but often his mount is tired or recalcitrant, and this obliges him, despite himself, to return to the ancient system. He also fights against second-class citizenship and forced labor. He is a true victim of colonial contradictions and declares himself in the name of this reasoning: what good does it do to recondition human mechanisms if you're going to turn right around and throw them out of gear with slavery? This involuntary complicity torments him. The only result of all his protestations was to cause him to be undesirable everywhere. Here he is, in exile in this village somewhere in Haute-Provence when, at his age, he should be directing urban conscription at home, or waiting for retirement in a ministry, interrogating cowries, like so many others.

The schoolmaster is the most striking figure, in Anatole's eyes, in the literal as well as the metaphorical sense. He educates and punishes with the same zeal, so effectively that one comes out from under his wing with a head full of knowledge and swollen with blows that are no less so. The history of Baoulia, made up of heroic battles, distant and glorious annexionist campaigns, and dates to remember, is inculcated with a heavy hand. The great crusades against the South African barbarians take up most of the curriculum which ends with the apotheosis of the (alas! only temporary) extermination of the infidels at the bridge on the river Kwai, at the time of the eighth crusade led by Queen Koumba the Fifth herself, assisted by Commander in Chief Ibra-Hima, the power behind the Transhumants.

The marabout initiated Anatole into the mysteries of religion and the moral principles of society. The one, almighty god is the Baobab which does not, nor ever has, grown in Europe. This is a sign that the continent has no divine essence. But the generosity of Baoulia is remedying this little by little: every village of Baoulian Western Europe has a sacred hothouse, thus it is true that "the shadow of the Baobab shelters all men regardless of color," and that the "Baobab deigns to put down its roots in every land where man implores aid and protection" . . .

How far away it all seems after a day in Bantouville! Overwhelmed by events, instantly subjected to the teeming aggressiveness of this crazy city, Anatole has not even had the opportunity to look over his fellow citizens. Nor, for that matter, have they had much chance to look him over, since, for the most part, all they have seen of him is his back in his desperate attempt to put some distance between his pursuers and himself. He would even have had a hard time describing, if not recognizing, this woman who harbors him, and with whom he has attained the limits of the imaginable.

After all, he has encountered only five types of Bantouvillians: the *Pigs,* who got him down, but wanted to get him good; the *Ants*, who taught him some facts of life by means of a porter; the *Chicks*: the ground-hostess at Amadou-Koumba station, then this girl from the Butte; all the rest are only *Low-lives* or *Rats*, the latter being the social category which he must consider his own from now on.

Here, the Low-Lives survive in every dive; the Pigs stamp you and cramp you, take a fall, but bust your balls; the Ants bubble in the rubble, grovel in their hovels, in rags and tatters, but it doesn't matter; the Chicks (black) don't look back, faces painted, slightly tainted, they prattle and tattle and shake their rattle; the Chicks (white) are ladies of the night, they show their wares, they don't care, they limp and scrimp to pay their pimp; the Rats hurry and scurry, chased by the cops until they drops. Could this be Bantouville, this anthill where everyone runs about with the speed of a gumbo going down a derelict's throat?

The door opens delicately. The young woman appears, craning her neck to see Anatole, who, wrapped in his thoughts, jumps like a child caught doing something naughty. In her arms she carries a tray full of food. "Hey, dude, you sleeping?"

The deferential word washes over Anatole like a balm, and in a flash he understands the outlaw that sleeps in the heart of every man, especially in the presence of a glowing bitch. So he answers with a kind of affectionate severity:

"You'd be stuck if I said yes, wouldn't you?"

She sets down the tray, then throws herself at her dude's neck without a word. She smells damn good, this little lady, she has a natural, peppery smell which does not leave Anatole unmoved, he who has been olfactory since day one. And the new outlaw becomes another kind of hard guy. If he let himself go . . . ! But the young woman unwraps herself to go turn on the light, and the impulse dwindles.

"I was just asking myself if there was any grub in these digs!" he says, pulling the providential tray across his thighs in an attempt to save face.

"I brought you the morning paper, too. Strange, though, it doesn't say anything about a toubab chased into the Butte . . . "

"So? Why should it? What are you trying to find out?"

"Don't get mad! All I said . . . I'm not nosy you know. I didn't even ask you your name."

"Neither did I."

"My name is Maggy. Like it?"

"Maggy what?"

"No what. Just Maggy. And you?"

She should have been called Maggy Sweetbuns, given her well-packed chassis. With a supercharged money-maker in back and a pair of shock-absorbant bumpers over her heart, she had a body like Bora Belkoukoune. This is not a niggardly compliment when one recalls the star's celebrated lumbar curve. It's simple. Moko Zombi himself, the unquestioned dictator of Baoul-Bledian (and therefore, universal) fashion claims that an imaginary line (if it was up to him, this line would be instead one of man's most real segments) drawn tangentially to the curve of her ass and the tip of her tits precisely intersects the navel of B.B.! With all due respect, a similar line on the proper orbit on Maggy would not miss this vital and strategic knot by much.

Anatole is so aware of this that he is disturbed, and without thinking gives his name. And he realizes, too late, that Maggy has the advantage.

"Well I have a first name *and* a last name: Anatole Dupont!"

At these words, Maggy falls onto the bed laughing. And with good reason: Bantouville is teeming with Duponts to the point that it is, so to speak, the ideal anonymous name.

"You can laugh all you want. In any case there are at least two real Duponts in Bantouville, my uncle Edgar and me. Whereas Maggy. . . ."

She stops short. Something has just happened: two strangers used to a laborious dialogue of gestures and monosyllables in a borrowed language, suddenly discover that they speak the same dialect.

"Did you say Edgar Dupont? The labor leader from Rue Birago?"

"That's him. I was going to go see him yesterday, before that patrol got on my bubu. But where do you know him from?"

The day before, she had been pretty sure that Anatole was not just anybody. Well her instincts were right! Edgar Dupont's nephew! Nothing less! Edgar Dupont, who's thick with the Archduke and who plotted Escartefigue's escape plan.

"I asked you a question! How do you know Edgar Dupont?"

But Maggy is straightaway on guard, and she shuts up. She has seen so much on the Butte! What if it's a trap by the notorious Inspector General Bozambo who has riddled the city with informers and cops disguised as Rats?

"Finish your breakfast," she says, "then we're going to go see someone."

2

The little streets which snake from Place Léon G. Soumaké to the assault of the Butte Mozamba, assume with the morning twilight, the effervescence of the true medina. The picturesque Butte which the tourists so enjoy, does not really come to life until nightfall, after the last thanksgiving prayers to the almighty Baobab, which has been transplanted into the Basilica, an artificial source of heat and humidity.

At this early morning hour, ritis, koras and balafons are put away for the time being and the streets belong to the fatous* and the toubab *boys*. This does not imply that the atmosphere stills. On the contrary! When, in front of every stall, a costermonger, his chechia at a rakish angle, scarf knotted to one side, and cigarette butt dancing in his mouth, when one of these is quarelling about cauliflowers, endives and green beans with some demanding customer, with a screaming infant slung on one hip, no Abomey tom-tom could hope to cover their voices. This is the usual in the native markets: bartering, arguments, fistfights sometimes. So much so that many Bantouvillians prefer to shop at the supermarkets where the poultry and vegetables imported from Baoulia are more expensive, but undergo a strict pricing and are packed in cellophane.

At the moment that Maggy and Anatole are coming out at one end of Rue Alioune-the-Elusive, the sounds of a bitter conjugal dispute meets them head on. A gracious shrew is going at her concubine. Neither is visible, but you don't have to have second sight to picture the mustached virago, fat-assed and pot-bellied, blunt instrument in one hand, planted firmly in front of some poor puny bugger, who is huddled up, already vanquished by her invective.

---

*Housemaids

"So you don't feel like working! In the sack you always claim to be tired! What are you waiting for? Why don't you just cut out with someone else, you jellyfish?" she screams.

"I'm just too tired. Ya hear that, mama? I'm just too tired even to split!" whimpers this castrato piteously.

A crowd has gathered on the sidewalk, and the rubberneckers are jostling each other in front of the window to catch the whole show. Not one charitable soul comes to the aid of this male, at the mercy of this enraged praying mantis. On the contrary, jeers break out in the crowd.

"Watch it, or you'll lose your daily bread, baby! Get what you want from your old man, that's what he's for!"

"If he hollers, let him go!" advises another, who knows his classics.

"Hey, come on! It's not his fault if he can't get it up!"

"Throw down a bar of soap! If he picks it up, you'll know for sure, Honey!"

"Yeah? And your mother!" explodes Honey, leaping to the window.

"My mother pisses on you!"

"That's funny! I thought she busted her pisser on the job!"

Anatole would like to hear more, but Maggy, who no doubt has had her fill of this kind of entertainment, a common one in this part of town, takes him by the sleeve and drags him away.

There is a parking lot just behind Mozambo cemetery. It is, in fact, a sort of cemetery for cars, adjoining the one for people. Abandoned metal carcasses rot in garbage-filled corners. They are not all abandoned: one can see smoke rising here, rags on a clothes-line fluttering there.

Maggy goes unhesitatingly towards a thirty-zebu-power, pre-war model Derlin-Zinsou, a double-decker bus which stands out like a mansion in this extraordinary shantytown. The tenant is obviously an aristocrat. Suprisingly a brand-new horn hangs from the stanchion of the cockpit. Its windows are intact and with the net curtains on the inside it resembles a most respectable foyer. Maggy squeezes the horn and honks five times: beepbeepbeep-beepbeep! Three short, two long. That is, three white and two black, in keeping with Baoulian musicology which stipulates that one black equals two whites. Then she whistles the first bars of "I'm proud to be a Bambara . . . ," an unusual song, certainly, for the nationalist toubabs, but one which can be sung in the beards of the African cops without arousing suspicion.

Almost immediately, a bean-pole, just awakened with everything unbuttoned, appears from the direction one would least have expected. A several-days' beard bristles on his gaunt cheeks while from under the rim of his naval petty officer's cap, emerge a few tufts of scrubby blond hair.

"Oh, it's you, little one!" he announces. His lively little eyes dart furtively towards Anatole from the recesses of startlingly sunken sockets: "Whozzat?"

"Can we come in?" she asks, "*This friend brings news of your grandfather!*"

This last phrase is a password of course. Since the man she is addressing is at least a grandfather himself, it would be unlikely that he could be the grandson of anyone who could still get it on.

"Oh, okay," he says, "I was wondering what would bring anybody here this early."

They disappear into the mansion-bus. Maggy and the man discuss Anatole, but not with Anatole. So he listens, and his expression is so tense, so preoccupied that he is almost pitiful.

"Dju hear about a guy who was chased into the Butte yesterday?" she asks.

"That him? I heard you'd gone off with . . . What's his name?"

"Anatole Dupont."

"What? Who're you kidding?"

"Honest! That's what he told me. Seems Edgar from Rue Birago is his uncle."

"Well, I'll be damned!"

Only then does he condescend to look at Anatole. After examining him, he says: "Okay, how do I know you're Edgar's nephew?"

"But he really is my uncle!" protests Anatole.

"Can you prove it?"

"What do you mean-proof? Should I have let the infantry catch me?"

"Listen to him, will ya? 'Should I have . . .'" His honor talks like a book. Listen, pal, that's your business. Are you or aren't you Edgar's nephew?"

"Here are my papers. Pick one, any one."

The contents of Anatole's pockets are spread out on the table: certificate of baptism; circulation permit; certificate of good character, in short, all the documents he has laboriously assembled for his entry into Bantouville. Unbending, the aristocrat continues with a disdainful air:

"This is all Baoulian bric-a-brac. What does it prove? Don't prove shit, all the undercovs have them."

"And this," says Anatole, "My father gave it to me for Uncle Edgar. Look!"

The envelope isn't sealed. The man grabs it, pulls out a clumsily scribbled sheet and begins to read without stopping for breath.

"Hey," he says, "is this a joke, or what? I'm warning you, all I have to do is honk a certain way and you'll see two bruisers show up who don't have much of a sense of humor. And then it'll be too bad for you, Totole!"

Maggy joins them, takes the letter out of his hand and reads it in her turn.

"Maybe it's all true," she says.

"You think so? Okay, we'll forward this letter! You know where Uncle Edgar is now? At the Building, getting grilled. Understand?"

Again, Anatole protests, "But I swear. . . . "

"In a pig's eye!" interrupts the man, sealing the letter. "Maggy, go mail this right now. And write on the envelope: 'Care of Inspector General Bozambo, Federal Building'. Don't bother sticking on B.B.'s map. It's interoffice."

Maggy, seriously shaken, prepares to go. She gives Anatole a long inquiring look. No, she isn't mistaken about him. She adds, her hand on the latch:

"As far as I'm concerned, Anatole is okay. I think you're barking up the wrong tree, Archduke!"

3

So this bewildering, stubborn old mule is none other than the Archduke! What Federal inspector, not very inclined toward venturing into the medina, would suspect this strange man in this automobile graveyard of being the yellow eminence of subversive activity? Even the natives who live in contact with him wouldn't divine his secret identity. It must be said that this fellow has managed to create, very successfully, by his innocuous physical appearance, his fanciful costume, and his common language, added to an innate sense of theater, the character of a mild-mannered carwasher. Everyone on the Butte knows Prosper Yoplaboume—his official binomial—they confide in him, put up with his eccentricities, leave him the car keys, reward him with generous tips. But no one knows that he puts all those confidences to use, that, in fact, he has instigated them more than once, and that he never neglects to examine the contents of the glove compartments carefully. The consequent inventory says as much about the driver as a handbag does about a society woman. Moreover, you find the most surprising things scattered in there: dentures, aphrodisiac pills, new and second-hand Zambian letters, extra pairs of women's panties and sanitary napkins, illustrated playing cards to be kept out of the children's hands, guinean cup-and-balls, chewed kola nuts, bilingual Baoulian-Gallic baobabist breviaries, a glass eye, and to top it all, an item undoubtedly unique of its kind: a transistorized hottentot dildo in genuine ebony.

Inspector General Bozambo believes that a study should be done on the careers of those of the colonizes who live off the regime. With all due respect, the careers of those who don't—whether because of ideology or circumstance—would also be worth a glance. And that of the Archduke, alias Prosper Yoplaboume, is both informative and colorful.

Born on the Butte, he remained an only child

after the premature death of his father who was unable to survive a wild shot by an outlaw who was being pursued by the police. Now, the deceased certainly never worked like a honky, but the household managed to live on his earnings, of which no one ever questioned the source. Following the tragedy, his widow, having received no compensation for damages, sought an indemnity from the State. It was amply demonstrated to her that the State, on the one hand, had no obligation toward her, since the fatal shot was not fired by one of its agents, and that she could expect no compensation from the killer on the other hand, since he had ultimately been killed himself and there was nothing to indicate his financial position, nor that of his heirs who had not appeared at the morgue. Very fortunately, the orphan's grandfather, a petty officer in the national navy, posted with his unit in Baoulia, agreed to allocate a transfer of pay to his daughter-in-law. Thus, from his earliest youth, Prosper held a deep devotion toward Petty Officer Yoplaboume.

When he came of age, he was further traumatized by two events which occurred almost simultaneously: his mother's death, due to the aftereffects of a youthful indiscretion, and his grandfather's return, heavily decorated, but retired without pension. The roles became reversed: Prosper now supported the ex-military man. Business was not too bad: blessed with a well-developed physique and popular with the ladies, he had become a sort of king of the streets.

The grandfather, a former basket-weaver, found work with a wine merchant weaving straw covers for demi-johns, on the Rue Marteau-qui-Cogne. However, the disability which had brought about his discharge soon proved itself incompatible with this providential employment. He had a godi-massa, what the great medical minds of the Baoulian Faculty describe as elephantiasis of the scrotum or Zogo-Massey's disease. This scourge is apparently transmitted by mosquito bites in Africa: after a few months one begins to swell surreptitiously in one part of the body or another: in women the breasts, in men the privates, in both, the legs. It becomes gigantic, inhuman. Try to hold a demi-john between your knees when that vital space is already occupied by such a monstrosity!

Most unfortunate of all, for all that Prosper kept at the daily grind, his affairs were in a bad way and so, to avoid the dishonor of failure, he chose to sell his goodwill to a colleague, who was even more of a hustler than himself. Through a real tour-de-force, however, he had never had any trouble with the police. He had never once been held for questioning, nor left the city; there was no dossier in his name, not a fingerprint existed in the files of the Federal Police. It was not until much later that he came to realize the advantage to be drawn from this privileged situation: who could be a more effective subversive agent than someone with a clean record?

As for Petty Officer Yoplaboume, his job possibilities, as well as the possiblities of orders to Barbados diminished as the family jewels swelled. He stayed home, battleweary, passing long hours recounting his adventures in the mother country, and his many heroic deeds which reinforced his grateful but ever hopelessly unemployed grandson's admiration for him.

About that time, the colonial authorities decided to undertake a massive restoration of the Butte Mozamba basilica. There was wholesale recruiting of native labor. Prosper and his grandfather were among these and were thus able to establish their first physical contact with the proletariat. They encountered a veritable army of down-and-outs, of whom Edgar Dupont was one, all solidly flanked by politico-labor leaders, such as Escartefigue, who took turns passing the good word and distributing pamphlets from bubu to bubu, around the work-site.

A spark struck instantly between Escartefigue and Prosper. The Bantouvillian labor leader rapidly convinced the other that, until colonialism was brought down, all healthy males ran the risk of finding themselves in the line of fire of a fatal bullet, like Prosper's father, or in that of a diseased mosquito, like his grandfather. Prosper turned out to be a remarkable agent, both disciplined and full of initiative, which is not common. And so it was natural that he should come to be called, in the greatest secret, Escartefigue's heir apparent.

The work was at its height around the Basilica. Prosper had discovered in himself, pick in hand, an aptitude for physical labor, at the same time that he had committed himself to an ideology. No one put as much soul into demolition as he. His grandfather's job was to take the rubble in a wheelbarrow to a large pit which had to be filled. This was not easy, considering his infirmity. But they say that work ennobles a man and stimulates his intellect. The ex-Petty Officer adapted to the situation ingeniously. He began by filling the wheelbarrow by great spadefuls; when it was full, he insinuated himself carefully between the handle-shafts, took up the skirt of his bubu in both hands, hoisted his enormity into the vehicle and set off. When he got to the edge of the pit, he unloaded his testicles, shook out the wheelbarrow and that was that. Who could ask for better?

But one day, tragedy brutally struck the work-site. How true it is that, even ennobled by his work, an old man remains at the mercy of the vagaries of his memory. And so it came to pass that Grandpa Yoplaboume, certainly rendered careless by fatigue, forgot that day to haul in his privates. He was never to know that this trip was to be his last, for he paid for this ill-timed distraction with his life.

When the overly-weighted wheelbarrow began its usual gyratory movement, the centrifugal force, the force of gravity, all the forces of nature which were lying in wait, worked together to precipitate the load into the abyss. The unfortunate man, despite being covered by his bubu as by a parachute (it twisted up anyway) didn't stand a chance of landing at the bottom of the pit after the rubble, so heavy was his godi-massa. The enormous elephantiasic mass headed straight toward the nadir, like a several-megaton bomb, carrying with it its owner's thin body. He screamed fit to wake the dead, but remained absolutely rigid, maintaining despite himself a perfectly aerodynamic posture. At the terminus, the rubble lapidated Yoplaboume, and the wheelbarrow crushed him before covering him in its turn. And so it was that he breathed his last, to all intents and purposes walled in, *in camera*, as it were.

This incident completed Prosper's transformation. This huge, devouring, monstrous thing which with gravity's complicity had destroyed his beloved grandfather, would always stand between Baoulia and himself. He withdrew from the world and went to live in the carcass of a bus, a stone's throw from the cemetery, determined not to move from there even under fire. And so he became a carwasher, wearing that sempiternal sailor's cap, inherited from the Petty Officer. In this way the years passed until the day Escartefigue was offered a well-earned rest on the damp straw of a prison cell. Then Prosper Yoplaboume was forced to reveal his secret identity to the initiated. The Archduke entered the scene.

Chapter Four

1

At Champs-Baobabs Circle which Avenue Tonton Makoute crosses not far from the Federal Building, the newspaper sellers are carrying on more than usual. About ten of them are announcing at high volume the sensational headline which stands out in bold type on the front page. The liberal *Universe*; the conservative *Shearer*; the reactionary *Twilight*; the clerical-progressive *Baobabist Monitor*; all, despite their ideological differences, have plagiarized each other shamelessly, joining *The Baoulia News*, the gossip-mongers' favorite rag, and announce in chorus: **New subversive gang in Bantouville. Brilliant intervention by the bomb squad against saboteurs.**

Taken aback, the passersby—almost exclusively Black in this fashionable neighborhood—stop, reach into their pockets, grab the papers and take off without waiting for their change. Bursts of exclamations. Real consternation. The affair is recounted in such a melodramatic tone that each reader, becoming suddenly aware of the danger he has escaped, feels all the more admiration for the valiant Baoulian army, and indignation toward the ungrateful, criminal natives.

This unusual animation at Champs-Baobabs Circle reaches Bozambo who has opened wide his windows to let some air into his stuffy office. He realizes immediately that something out of the ordinary has occurred. The newspaper vendors have never made such a racket, except on the day after the launch of the first Bambara astronaut, or following the famous speech by President Moktar Alas on Corsican self-determination.

He buzzes to find out what it's all about. Constance appears forthwith.

"Go down and get me the papers!" he says, throwing her a thousand-baoul bill.

"Which?"

"All of them . . . Hey! Let me see that!"

Constance returns the bill which he examines carefully against the light.

"Aha! I thought so! You can tell your little pals, the vendors, that the job's already been done! The Witch Doctor's eye is out! Go on, take it and get out!"

Once again alone, he asks himself who could have passed him this desecrated bill. It couldn't have been Frederick who only gives him back small change, and even then, since that rascal makes a little on the side, it's rare that he gets anything back after shopping. No, it must have been a Negro, a friend—or someone who pretends to be a friend. Suddenly he knows, and cannot repress a shout.

"How about that! Adiami! Commander Adiami! That boar! Day before yesterday he gave me five one thousand-baoul bills for a five-thousand! You swine, you'll get yours!"

The hubbub on the street increases and tears him from his thoughts of revenge. "Things must be getting pretty hot in Corsica," he thinks.

There have been rumors lately of negotiation, but these peace rumors have turned out to be without foundation, so to speak. They even pointed to the secret discussions between the Maghrebin representatives and the leaders of the rebellion. Only the *Plucked Toucan*, the satirical weekly, often seized by the government (but whose information has never been disproved) judges that "we can't be believin' that the army'll be leavin'." The Maghrebin army is violently opposed to any non-military solution, but it can't seem to crush the Corsican fellagha. Having lost ground with a failed putsch, with counter-terrorist operations, and fake attempts on the life of President Alas, whom it had put in power in the first place, the army is discredited in the eyes of many Maghrebins, those with full citizenship, as well as the others, and certain of its leaders are holed up in a fortress at Ras-el-Melah. As for Alas, he keeps a haughty distance from it, and has not deigned to visit Corsica since his last tour of the Canary Islands, during the course of which he ate couscous with his officers and attended an unforgettable country malouf*. There are those who say

*Concert of Maghrebin music

he is afraid. But Moktar Alas is not the man to fear violent death. He has proved it time and again on the occasion of many official visits across the Maghreb, where he did not hesitate to leave the chimps in charge of security to go mingle with the delirious throngs riddled with provocateurs and anarchists . . .

Constance throws a bundle of newspapers on the desk, looks at her boss with pointed emphasis and declares:

"My little pals wouldn't take your Witch-Doctor. I am returning it. I paid for the papers myself. . . ."

She turns to go without asking to be paid back. The Chief of Territorial Security's yelp stops her in mid-swivel. The pose is a pretty one, both enigmatic and provocative, and this does not help to restore Bozambo's calm.

"What do you mean they wouldn't take it? What right do they have?"

"Come on, sir! You know very well that these one-eyed bills are worthless, and that any person who brings them to a bank is liable to a three-to-six month prison sentence. You yourself suggested the measure to the Governor General of the O.B.E. . . ."

"Okay, okay! That's enough out of you! Speak when spoken to!"

"Yes, sir!"

"Furthermore, the last thing I want is to owe

you anything. I'm paying you back right now!" says Bozambo furiously, pulling his wallet from the inside pocket of his bubu.

The bills are spread out on the table. Bozambo examines them rapidly one by one, and his face expresses every emotion imaginable, from astonishment to a furious rage.

"Holy Baobab! All my Witch Doctors have an eye out!"

Constance bursts out laughing, and, deliberately turning her back on her employer who is now on the verge of apoplexy, jeers at him as she walks out the door:

"Six months in jail! Six months in jail!. . . ."

He jumps to his feet, hurling himself towards her, but she has already disappeared down the hall. So he slams the door and proceeds to beat his fists against it. He rests leaning against the jamb for a moment, panting with fury and resentment. A kola nut helps, chewed with cannibal hatred. After a few minutes, Bozambo feels better and returns to his desk, but his throat tightens again when he unfolds *The Baoulia News*;

"By the hippo's prostate!" he bawls, "I've had it up to here with these coconut reporters and these gabby officers! Adiami. . . ."

His threat remains in mid-air, since he isn't altogether sure what he wants to do to Commander Adiami, other than strangle him on the spot.

"He's not going to put anything over on me! I'll tell the Governor if I have to!"

The *Baoulia News* reporter has broached his tale in the style of a baoul-store detective novel:

"A run-of-the-mill incident which happened to a native infantry patrol has set off a serious matter which threatens the security of the State. In reality the affair began much earlier and only the well-known astuteness of our bright star, Commander Adiami, made it possible for the first threads of a subversive network to be tied together.

A few days ago, for no apparent reason (the plant had been inspected during summering), the boiler of the Federal Building exploded. Arriving immediately on the scene, the illustrious head of the bomb squad, thanks to his usual keen sense of smell, detected in the air the odor of explosive plastic. At first, no one believed it, least of all the lights of the D.T.S. who, unable to accept the idea of sabotage within their own building, claimed it was an accident attributable to excessive pressure. It was not long before the facts proved them wrong, and two days later, in a pamphlet which was rapidly intercepted, the Archduke claimed credit for the outrage."

"This is news to me," sighs Bozambo.

And yet this pamphlet really was intercepted. The Director of General Information, who does not believe in the existence of the Archduke and who seized the printed matter, chose not to inform Bozambo for fear that he might rejoice as he does at every sign of the new leader of the Gallic A.C.M.

Bozambo has never been so angry for so long. He keeps on reading but learns nothing more as sensational, the *Baoulia News* chronicler's information supports what he has already heard from his friend Colonel Sar. He lingers, however, over two items which have wounded him deeply: the stupidity of which he is accused by the liberal as well as the reactionary reporters for not believing in the explosive, and this story of the pamphlets about which he knows nothing.

They need a token scapemerino to distract from the failures of the powers-that-be, he thinks, and he's been elected. There can be no other explanation for the mysteries and accusations of which he is a victim. He is on someone's white list.

Even his special detectives are shirking their work these days. They complain of being exhausted. It has been four days since they were assigned to Edgar Dupont's domicile and there has been no positive result. As far as that goes, they would be hard pressed to identify the individual whom they have seen only through a spy-hole and that for only a few minutes before he was summarily thrown out of the building by the inspectors who were interrogating him. They had seen a sort of gargoyle on a stool, and had taken the opportunity to express some reservations about the possibility of recognizing Dupont in the future. So some criminal dossiers were produced and that confused them completely.

Since then, they have been keeping an eye on the house around the clock, but they haven't seen him go in or out and, without sharing their doubts with Bozambo, they wonder if perhaps Dupont hasn't shaken them. But Dupont isn't as white as he is painted. And this is just the beginning.

Yes, this is just the beginning, because here is today's mail on Inspector General Bozambo's desk. In no time at all he has located among the official correspondence, a handwritten envelope addressed to Edgar Dupont, care of himself. And look, no stamp! Unpleasant as it is, this certainly deliberate omission is, all things considered, not as humiliating as a caricature of the celebrated international star would have been. As for the origin of the letter, it's as clear as day: another coup by the patriot toubabs who wrack their brains trying to tie his nerves in knots. Grabbing a paperknife, he opens the envelope with one brusque movement. His heart seems to stop when he reads the brief message which mentions neither date nor place:

"My dear Edgar:

The grape harvest hasn't been too bad, but it's not as you knew it before the war. I haven't gotten anything back from the cooperative yet. I'll send you ten thousand baouls as soon as possible. In the meantime, please take in Anatole as we agreed; when there's enough for ten, there's enough for eleven.

He has some nice pomegranates from our orchard for the children.

Your loving brother,
Marius"

Don't even try to knock at the Inspector's door, or to phone him. It is unlikely that he will answer since, after howling Adiami's name, his head has begun to swim and, with a sob, he is now beating his head on his crocodile-skin desk pad.

It is by chance that Constance, come to get the mail to be filed, discovers her boss, his skull lying nervelessly on his desk, propped up on a pile of newspapers, his part almost vertical on his head, a sheet of notebook paper in his hand. She thinks he is napping, so she calls him softly at first, prepared to face his temper at being discovered thus. No response. Going closer, she sees that he does not look normal. Suddenly, she is disturbed, and wonders. Heart attack? Assassination! The hell with protocol! She grabs him by the shoulders and shakes him.

"Inspector General! Mister Bozambo! Are you dead? Answer me!"

A low growl rises from the Bozambian depths, carrying with it the certainty that the person is alive and well. What's more, he speaks, and in the future tense, and in threats.

"Adiami, I'll get you! You'll pay for this if it kills me, you bastard!"

"Here, drink this!" says Constance, having quickly procured a glass of water.

Bozambo, somewhat recovered, feels vaguely the touch of a soft, warm hand on his nape, on his face the soothing caress of a fruity-smelling breath. He lets himself go. He drinks but unfortunately swallows the wrong way. He coughs, splutters, hawks, swears, curses, abuses, pales, coughs again, sneezes, sniffs, blows a disgusting excretion out through his irritated nostrils. Nauseated by this revolting display, Constance has executed a prudent retreat, and waits some ten paces away, holding the glass precariously in her damp fingers.

"Go on, get out!" says Bozambo peremptorily, his eyes glaring over the edge of some kind of kerchief he has pulled from somewhere and is now holding in front of his face.

He blows his nose in resounding glissandos, and Constance takes advantage of this to exclaim:

"What do you mean, get out! Is this the thanks I get?"

"Thanks for what?"

"For bringing you 'round."

"Me? Bringing me 'round? Are you dreaming, my girl?"

"I may be dreaming, but you're the one who was sleeping!"

And with that, she leaves, slamming the door once more. As a result of the shock wave, the portrait of President Mango Zekodene which hangs over Bozambo's armchair, wobbles perilously. We may expect it to fall one of these days and give the Inspector another part, or scalp him with a shard of glass, even kill him, in which case he would have the great honor of dying at his post, in the exercise of his duties.

2

When Colonel Sar, anxious to get to dinner with his native sweetheart, had entrusted the Dupont case to his adjutant, Commander Adiami, the latter, who had been sniffing after a glorious deed for some time, had jumped at the chance. The opportunity to win points, to prove once and for all that Bantouvillian subversive activity was entering a new phase, and an explosive one at that was too good. The conflagration at Amadou-Koumba station, the one that had blown up the heating plant at the Federal Building, and the contents of the suitcase abandoned by a fugitive, not far from Boulevard Sékou, must all be seen as the actions of a single group.

The reasoning was a small masterpiece of bad faith since Adiami was in a position to know that the coup at the station had been perpetrated by the Pale Hand, discreetly armed and supported by his own staff; that there was no definite proof that the explosion in the Building was of a criminal nature; and that the suitcase had not yet revealed its secrets.

He picked up the receiver and dialed the number of the laboratory.

"This is Commander Adiami. Let me speak to Sergeant Makoko."

"Speaking, Commander."

"So what's in that damned package for Edgar Dupont?"

"We drew a blank, Commander."

"What do you mean?"

"We found about a dozen toubab fruits. I opened them all, cut each one up. It's real fruit, Commander."

"Fruit?"

"Yes, Commander. Consequently a familial gift."

"Oh, spare me your jargon, will you? What kind of fruit is it?"

"I am uninformed as to the nature of the fruit. I've never seen anything like them in Baoulia."

"Okay, you idiot, I'm coming down to see!"

Downstairs, Adiami found himself brought up short at the sight of a kind of fruit salad, the result of his subordinate's zealous investigation.

"Pomegranates!"

"But Commander, with all due respect, grenades are . . . metallic."

At the sergeant's astonishment, Adiami immediately realized that nothing was lost. Grenades! What a providential misunderstanding to exploit.

Clapping the sergeant's shoulder authoritatively, he continued:

"Yes, you're right. But these are grenades too. Life is beautiful, Makoko!"

Then, forsaking the elevator, he ran up the stairs four at a time, leaped to the phone to call a reporter friend of his–and thence the sensational release in all the Baoulian newspapers three days later.

But he had figured without the accompanying letter and the Archduke's initiative. The machinery which had been so well set in motion was to stall soon, simply because, unbeknownst to Adiami, the matter of the one-eyed bills, intended as a mere practical joke, had coincided with the press release and the arrival of Dupont's letter in Bozambo's hands.

Because for Bozambo there is no longer any Dupont affair. The only matter of any importance now is the Adiami affair, and the motivation behind that is very clear: a coup at the expense of the D.T.S. and its chief. They have tried to make a fool of him, to make him look like a dumb, unimaginative cop. But they went too far, and someone adroitly put him in the know. This shrewd move was, in his opinion, the work of Colonel Sar, as anxious to clear the name of a childhood friend (hadn't they, not so long ago, worn out their bubus together on the seats of Béhanzin-the-Great high school?), as he was to avoid alienating a pushy busy-body of a deputy.

That's it, he's got the right fix on it now! A gimmick, a sure scheme, that couldn't possibly fail. Adiami is the kind of opponent you just don't play around with. One shouldn't pounce except with the surety of winning, of sinking him once and for all. A tough target—and all the more since Bozambo, an intelligent type but of no range, is absolutely lacking in imagination. For here it is hardly a matter of trumping up "proofs" against some accused native. This prey is of another species altogether—and capable of a ferocious resistance. So Bozambo knew he could get cut up himself if he didn't take care.

Just the same, could a guy swallow all the provocations of the deputy commandant without striking back? The only response to such a question is to launch an attack immediately which would be all the more stunning for its surprise—like the hot coal in the dull ashes. To start, Bozambo set himself to put a watch on Adiami day and night: at his office, his home, the public places he visits—all to be under constant surveillance by the Federal Secret Police. And the "reason": ah, the junior commandant had to be protected (discreetly of course, but effectively) against threats of death received from the nationalist toubabs. By Baobab, something good will turn up, or his name wasn't Bozambo.

3

In the odorous autobus, Anatole began to feel

time drag heavily. One could catch the ripe man here, from the usual male mess to the carelessness of an occupant obviously used to the acrid perfume of dirty linen, cold tobacco smoke, and a wide open garbage can–aromas which not even a whiff of antiseptic could dominate. This demonic man, the Archduke, who didn't even bother to be offended by the last words of Maggy, puttered around with household concerns, paying no attention to Anatole who was studying him with a dubious look. Now, turning on the gas to boil a pan of water, the Archduke carefully prepared some coffee to the tune of a constant clicking of his tongue, possibly caused by the fretting of a broken tooth or a poorly done dental job.

"You want a shot?" he questioned, the pan suspended just above the coffee pot.

"No thanks," murmured Anatole, "I've already eaten."

"You had it at Maggy's? A true momma-hen, that cutie."

Anatole kept quiet, all the more since he really had nothing to say–and the Archduke could keep the "dialogue" to himself.

"Why don't you say something?" demanded the Archduke again, his pointed cap always sitting on his strongly brachycephalic skull, the back of which was so flatly sloping as to have been conceivably shaped by the slice of an axe.

"I dunno."

"Then why don't you take off?"

"I dunno."

"Not very chatty, are ya? I dunno, I dunno. . . . "

"Where would I run away to? I've been running for two days. I don't know anyone here except Maggy, my uncle Edgar and you. I don't know where Maggy's gone. No news from my uncle. And you . . ."

"Go ahead, say it! What about me?"

"Doesn't matter," says Anatole, "I don't think you trust me."

"Trust! That's easy to say! All I have is your word. You know what that's worth? Just to start with, where do you come from? What's your act? I don't know anything about you. . . ."

Would Anatole be able to justify himself, to explain what he is, a student just off the boat from his native province, and who as yet had neither bed nor board in Bantouville? Perhaps after that they could begin to trust each other.

He didn't have the chance to tell his story. The warning system of the bus, wheezy and bi-tonal, suddenly honked five times, then, after a brief pause, someone whistled "I'm proud to be a Bambara."

"Shut up!" whispered the Archduke flatly, "I'll go see."

The old man slithered like an eel down a trap door in the rear platform of the vehicle and disappeared without a sound. Hoping for Maggy's return, Anatole went to peep through a crack and saw outside, bundled in a tired old bubu, a middle-aged toubab woman in kerchief and sunglasses. What could have possessed her to get herself up in shades like those in this morning mist rising from the meanders of the Sekouana! If she was an activist, her discretion left something to be desired, since there was little chance that her outfit would pass unnoticed.

Shortly thereafter she disappeared from Anatole's field of vision and in less time than it takes to tell reappeared in the bus at the hatch opening, with an agility as remarkable as that of the Archduke's who preceded her. Not very smart, maybe, but a pretty supple old lady.

Eh? What? Barely has she gotten to her feet, than here she is pouncing on Anatole, hugging him to the point of suffocation in her muscled arms, holding him to her breast, which is surprisingly flat and hard for a woman of her build, and says in a male and nicotined voice:

"Little one, how happy I am to find you here!"

Anatole is taken aback for a moment, looks at her, embarrassed, and suddenly cries: "Uncle!"

"A family's a funny thing! The uncle is an aunt!" The Archduke tried to sound sarcastic, but was rather sheepish after all.

After these brief demonstrations of affection, the leader of the Gallic A.C.M. regained his sense of priorities and Edgar Dupont told of his misadventures. After leaving the Federal Building precipitously, a broken man with a torn lip and a white eye, he stopped to pull himself together at a bar on the Butte where he had credit, and where he would have had a hard time increasing his credit if he'd shown up in his everyday face. They served him surprisingly quickly and, in pursuance of mozambian custom (which forbids questioning a beaten customer) no one seemed to notice his condition. Then he continued on his way home still unable to understand the reason behind this latest interrogation, and even less the reason behind its abrupt interruption. The only new element was the hazy stamp story. Certainly, it was more than enough to charge someone with; natives have ended up at the morgue for far less. But the inspector's aggressiveness, the important mechanism set in motion for the interrogation, were completely out of proportion with the alleged crime.

A few spans from his house, while taking a short cut to Rue Birago (this saved him in fact, since he wouldn't have had a chance if he'd been out in the open) he saw, hanging from his window a flag with the Baoulian colors. He stopped short and was tempted to go back, this piece of cloth being an agreed signal between his daughter and himself to warn him in case of danger.

But he had to find out what was going on. He moved forward cautiously, hugging the wall, taking advantage of the slightest recess and before long he saw two persons pacing back and forth in front of the house. Although they were toubabs, there was nothing about them to suggest they were from the neighborhood. On the contrary, with their regulation wool bubus, and rumpled raincoats over their shoulders—they must be sweating blood!—they reeked of cop a kilospan away. They could only be a special detail from the Federal Police.

All in all, he had thought, the Baoulian police wasn't very smart. To entrust domiciliary visits and the escorting of natives under arrest to African inspectors, while detailing white auxiliaries for tails and surveillances, as exhausting as they are dangerous: all this is standard colonial procedure. The duties of an inspector imply a prestige and a confidence which are inconceivable where the special police are concerned. They are bound to their prey by color, and are caught in a dilemma. They are condemned to serve with a cynicism and villainy which become fiercer all the time in order to serve their masters and earn their daily manioc. But to let these hated and clumsily-disguised puppets loose on the mozambian streets which teem with hardened criminals is to take the Bantouvillians for complete fools.

So Edgar Dupont left without waiting to see more. This persistence on the part of the Federal Police worried him, however. What had he done that was so serious? His first reaction was to go to the Archduke immediately and study the situation, but at that hour it was unlikely that the car-washer would be in his own vehicle. And after what he had seen, he couldn't just wander around the Butte and environs, all the more since he was beginning to be overcome with fatigue.

There lived nearby a buxom activist, who had become his mistress, and with whom he had managed to produce three more children (all, fortunately, dead at an early age). This proximity had always proved itself advantageous and had worked out well for Dupont, who was at times unemployed, at times in jail, and always afflicted with a raging sexual appetite which his legitimate wife, exhausted from working and from her numerous obstetrical performances, couldn't assuage. By an irony of fate, his successive sojourns in the Building or in jail, no matter how brief, left Dupont in an extraordinary state of seminal impatience which reached a paroxismic intensity when he was discharged. As for his mistress, she was as devoted to her body as she was to her ideology and, stirred by who knows what phylogenic atavism, fornication whetted her appetite and lachrymal glands to the point that she would run from her partner, still teary, to throw herself on some food. For his part, Dupont, who had probably inherited some reptiloid chromosome, was all the more turned on by the sight of this bare-assed ogress engaged in crocodilian mastication. Thus their encounters became a continuous to-and-fro from bed to larder and back again. In short, he went to her house that evening, refreshed himself, and spent the night. The next day at dawn it was, ironically, disguised as a woman, in some schmata that his friend had lent him, that this relentless sire appeared at the Archduke's.

"What do you think they want from me?" asked Dupont after he had told his story.

The Archduke answered evasively, "Oh, you know how it is with the pigs . . . "

"You don't think its because of the Escartefigue plan, do you?"

Not in the least inhibited by his nephew's presence, he launched straight into a matter of the highest priority: the plan for Escartefigue's escape. But the Archduke, ever cautious, wouldn't listen and cut him short.

"You planning to run around dressed like a broad much longer?"

And indeed Dupont, who had removed his sunglasses, and whose white eye was turning the color of a ripe plum, looked rather dubious, with his kerchief tied at the nape of his neck, and his flowered bubu. To tell the truth, he resembled rather a member of the confraternity of pirates, seated as he was on a keg, with a shiner that looked like an eye patch.

"I have a suit on underneath," he said, holding up his bubu to show his tucked-up pants-legs.

"Okay, so change."

While doing so, Dupont exchanged a few words with Anatole. After discussing the family, they broached the subject of his studies, and the plans for his lodging. The Archduke who had been listening interrupted authoritatively:

"There won't be any studies!"

"Why not?" asked Dupont.

"Why don't you tell Edgar that the cops were on your case yesterday in the neighborhood? If you think you can go to school after that, you're barking up the wrong tree, sonny! Go ahead, tell him."

So Anatole had to describe his odyssey: the arrival at the train station, the incident with the porter, the unkindness of a police officer, the pursuit by a patrol, the abandonment of his suitcase. At that point, the Archduke stopped him:

"What was in the bag?"

"Some clothes and a package for Uncle Edgar."

"A package? Was his name on it? His address?"

"Yes, I think so," admitted Anatole.

"That's it, then!" erupted the Archduke. "It's all this little turd's fault! The pigs cop the bag, find the package and split for your house, Edgar! Got it?"

"What was in this package?" asked Dupont.

"Some pomegranates."

"What?"

"Some fruit. For the kids," 'fessed Anatole.

"Oh, so that's what the letter was about?" said the Archduke.

Dupont broke in "What letter?" as he pulled his bubu over his head.

"A note from your brother. Know what I did with it? I sent it to Bozambo. That'll serve the motherfucker right. As for your nephew, I'm keeping him here with me. I need an assistant for my work."

Anatole is disturbed: "What work?"

"Car-washer, Mister Student! With your fabulous diploma!"

Chapter Five

1

Seated in his swivel chair, his legs stretched out on the telephone table, deliberately turning his back to the desk which is buried under a pile of paperwork, too reminiscent of the tiring, noisome daily tasks, Commander Adiami meditates and finds life beautiful. His eyes dwell on the portrait of President Mango Zekodene, but he does not see it: he is savouring this new twist of fate with delight. A friend from Baoulia, close to official circles, has just told him in confidence that his name is on the list which has been submitted for presidential approval for promotion to the rank of lieutenant-colonel. If all goes well—and why shouldn't it?—he will be able to celebrate simultaneously his thirtieth birthday and his accession to the fifth stripe, probably plumed, but certainly definitive, since from here on in he will be addressed as "Colonel."

He is well aware that this success is not due to the results he has obtained in Bantouville, since he is forever at odds with his superior, Colonel Sar, whose methods inspire nothing but disapproval in him. Adiami, a disciple of the great Field-Marshal Amoakonte-Deumo, is a believer in strong measures to impress and ultimately demoralize the native. Colonel Sar, on the other hand, sees colonialism as a venture which carries within it the seeds of its own obsolescence; that is, the political and social evolution of the Overseas Baoulian Territories and, in the long run, the creation of a commonwealth of almost sovereign states, in the wake of the mother country. As if it were even imaginable that these backward, divided, quarrelsome Europeans could ever govern themselves! Toubabs, for how long have you been under Baoulian rule? For two hundred years, right? Well, you can do two hundred more. That's how they should be spoken to.

Only a few years ago, Adiami reached his objectives through a succession of roundabout movements, circumventing the obstacles he encountered. Those days are gone for good since he became a minister's protegé. Now he no longer works around an obstacle, he pulverizes it, and proceeds on his way without looking back.

It happened in Baoul-Bled . . .

One day, in the lobby of the House of Parliament, the minister, who wore a monocle, passed a seductive young staff attachée. The slender young Negress, whose charms nevertheless filled her bubu most pleasingly, had that regal carriage and innocently lascivious sway of the hips that go straight to an honest man's heart, although that kind of honesty is not necessarily a ministerial quality.

When he got to his office, the minister immediately summoned his chief of staff. He went straight to the point. He gave such a precise description of the disturbing creature that his assistant—who had already noticed her and was looking forward to hanging her on his meat rack—identified her without hesitation. A discreet inquiry allowed him to ascertain that she was from a northern province, that she lived by herself, and that she was struggling with some major problems since the decision handed down by Her Excellency herself which had revoked the right to lodging for attachés.

"Please inform this person that I would like to have a talk with her!"

With passion's help, the meeting was short and effective. The young lady, accepting the post in its most literal sense, became the almost permanent personal attachée to the minister in the capacity of private secretary, residing in his house. Naive, as are many girls from the North, she had no idea what such an honor entailed.

She was foisted by her patron on a vigilant and suspicious wife, but one who knew how to take things with good grace. And so she moved permanently into a guest room and even shared the couple's meals. It was not long before she found out that the so-called administrative work that she was so desperately needed for didn't amount to much after all.

His Honor the Minister passed insomniac nights imagining this goddess stretched out in the altogether, only a few spans from his room.

Furthermore he had to suffer, every morning, the sounds of her bustling about in the bathroom: every splash of water, every clink of a jar of face cream or beauty lotion against a shelf struck him like a rapier stab. All this was exacerbated by the fact that when he awoke, his wife never failed to comment wonderingly:

"You tossed and turned all night. You work too hard, it's getting on your nerves!"

He would then grumble something vague, and jump exasperated out of bed.

One night he made up his mind. After listening carefully to his spouse's respiratory rhythm, to be sure that she was sound asleep, he slipped furtively into the shadows, and with a few cautious strides came to his protegée's door. Being a trusting young person, she hadn't locked it. The door creaked slightly on its hinges as he went in. The young woman awoke suddenly, turned on the light and stifled a cry when she saw His Excellency appear, monocle in place and scantily but unambiguously clad. Taking advantage of her surprise, he hastened to get down next to her, and to convince her thus that being a minister did not preclude being a man. There followed a sweet silent extended bout, which ended in a draw, excited them a lot, but left both parties unsatisfied.

What destiny caused his wife to wake up in turn? Not finding her husband by her side, she got up and went to look for him. After searching each room, including the catish*, she decided to knock on the secretary's door. Trapped, the man foolishly adopted the ostrich technique and hid under the sheets.

Dignified, despite the ouolove curlers which bristled with short tufts and divided her scalp into a precise grid, Her Excellency the Minister's wife exploded, served notice that the Egeria was over, and intimated to her spouse that he was to regain the nuptial chamber. She was as imperial in this as one of Lamine Zamba's heroines. Her rival, at a loss, remained speechless. But at that point, His Excellency rose from his hiding place and counter-attacked:

"Aminata, if you want a divorce you can have it!"

After this superb rejoinder, the minister, wrapped in his house bubu, adjusted his monocle and exited majestically (after the fashion of the ancients).

The ex-attachée went to tell her misfortunes to Adiami, at that time a captain and, like her, from the North. He listened for a long time, got a down payment in kind, and went in uniform to seek an audience at the ministry. There a stiff and formal bailiff, with a polished skull and chain-covered chest, after leaving Adiami to cool his heels, came and informed him that the minister regretted that he was unable to receive him but

---

*W.C.

that he would lend "a most attentive ear" to a written petition. Enraged, Adiami grabbed a piece of paper and wrote a simple phrase: "Aminata, if you want a divorce, you can have it." He slipped the sheet into an envelope, sealed it and gave it to the bailiff.

"I'll wait for the answer," he added.

A few seconds later he was ushered into the minister's office. The latter received him with outstretched hand and greeted him with extravagant demonstrations of cordiality.

"My dear friend! Delighted to see you! What can I do for you?"

And so it came to pass that shortly thereafter, Adiami was promoted to the rank of Commander, with an officer's stripe on his tongue, assigned forthwith to Bantouville . . .

After two years in the federal capital, life goes on, with the addition of yet another stripe. It is true that His Excellency as well has enjoyed a remarkable ascension. Today he is Minister of State and it is he who, should the occasion arise, would have the honor of taking over the duties of Prime Minister in an interim period. Since each session of the legislature opens with the same members and starts from there, he could well be the one to form the next government. So this would be an inopportune moment to slip on some banana peel and give the *Plucked Toucan* the opportunity to divulge to the Baoul-Bledians the tacky calimbery* which came to the ears of a shameless, ambitious officer, capable of the lowest blackmail.

As for the officer, he is thinking of other things. The immediate problem, in his eyes, is how to exploit the news of his imminent promotion right now. Fortunately, there is a correspondent for the Baoulian Press Agency who can refuse him nothing, although he has never condescended, so to speak, to honor her as he should with his many journalistic favors.

The ring of the phone interrupts his reverie, and although annoyed, he answers it automatically. The Secretary General of the Federal Government is calling. Their dialogue would have the great Laminè Zamba's ghost turning in its grave.

"Hello, Adiami?"

"Speaking."

The other identifies himself.

"Amoakonte-Deumo."

"Go ahead!"

"Tell me something! Do you know Bozambo well?"

"Maybe."

"Do you know that he's really got it in for you and he's talking about revenge? Do you know that?"

---

*Pantaloonery

"What do I care? That clown who's never had a two-eyed Witch Doctor pass through his hands! What does he want?"

"You should find out within a few days. Just wanted to let you know."

"I may be young, but some little cop's resentment can't touch the honor of an officer."

"That's all well and good. I'm glad to see your morale is up. Don't forget, forewarned is forearmed. Talk to you soon."

"Have faith in time, in my valour and in our laws."

No sooner has he finished with the secretary general than Adiami dials the number of the Baoulian Press Agency. He is calling a direct line so he gets his friend the reporter right away. She pales with pleasure at being sought out by this fascinating man.

He announces himself with:

"Hello, Seynabou the beautiful. Would you do your humble servant Adiami the honor of having lunch with him today?"

"What have I done to deserve this attention?"

"It's your charm, my gazelle. Say 'yes'."

"Okay."

"If you're good, you'll get a scoop, with, of course a few conditions, like before. Follow me?"

"My mouth is watering."

"Is it the menu or the scoop?"

"That remains to be seen."

"Is that blackmail?"

"Strategy, oh incorruptible one!"

2

The detectives of the Federal Police, assigned by Bozambo to survey Adiami's house have a feeling that something is about to happen at last.

When he got home, the commander sent his chauffeur away and it looked like a tip passed discreetly to the toubab corporal who, in return, treated his superior to an impeccable military salute. In the several days that they have been on this assignment, this is the first time they have witnessed this little business. Usually the corporal-chauffeur, after closing the gate, parks the car, goes into the villa by the service entrance and doesn't come out again until it is time to take the officer back to his office after the siesta. Thus it is time to be alert, since whenever someone is anxious to grease an open palm, it is always to impose on the owner of that hand the obligation to keep his eyes closed.

The mere prospect of not being bullied by Bozambo, as is the case after each negative report, is enough to make them forget their acid indigestion, exacerbated by great quantities of sandwiches swallowed in a hurry, to forget the cramps in their calves, cricks in their necks and other sorely tried corns and callouses.

Shortly thereafter they see a gleaming, late-model Derlin-Zinsou arrive, all white, at the steering wheel of which a splendid, elegant and skillfully made-up Negress is enthroned. The young woman is literally one with the car which acts as accessory to her contrasting outfit. The two men begin to hate the commander when, with a supple twist of the hips, she gets out of her seat, furling the skirt of her violet bubu piped with gold which reveals the curve of her copper calves and accentuates the rise of hips and bust. Ah! many happy returns, you bastard, enjoying yourself in there while we slave like honkies, exposed to the elements out here.

"Not a bad set of wheels!" says one.

"A 'Dugout'," declares the other, a connoisseur. "The latest creation of the national corporation. Mind you, the chick ain't bad either!"

"For sure! And for sure she's not here to play pishine."*

"In any case, she's not the one who's going to do him in, not the way the Boz means it, anyway!"

"Well, old man, some people don't risk acts of Baobab, eh? Seeing as how they've brought their work home . . . ."

"Baobab almighty! I wear a size 42, but I'd like to shove a forty-six at least up that N.C.O.'s ass!"

---

*In Gallic: to shoot craps

In the meantime the driver, who is none other than Seynabou the reporter, has propelled herself with a few efficient swings of the hip to the other side of the gate. Everything about her, from her hieratic way of carrying her head, to her feline way of walking, exemplifies a very Baoul-Bledian class. No doubt about it, this is a woman who is used to the smartest circles of the Baoulian capital, to receptions and fashion shows, and who probably draws a nice bundle of baouls at the end of each month (which never hurts), not counting the generosity of admirers who are prepared to ruin themselves for her.

The two detectives, the same who but lately worked over a certain Edgar Dupont, now reveal themselves to be perceptive psychologists, since their conjectures concerning the journalist come pretty close to the truth. Seynabou is more than comfortable materially and the object of much admiration, and not only in Bantouville. Motivated by that classical pattern in women, a spirit of contradiction, she despises those who worship her and adores those who, like Adiami, seem to despise her. For example, she has already tried more than one tactic with him. She has even gone so far to try and turn him on as to insinuate that he could be a soap-picker-upper. He got a good laugh out of that. And for good reason: but a few moments before he had had it tenderly out with a young dressmaker! For the truth is that only toubabesses move the commander. This is a common propensity among the intellectuals of the mother country who like to go slumming. The fact remains that today Seynabou is coming to visit with certain specific ulterior motives, which explains the particular care she has taken with her dress.

In the living room, Seynabou immediately takes over the role of lady of the house: she serves the cocktails, while in his armchair, he is sucking obstinately at his extinguished pipe. She has always found it abnormal that this young man, as intelligent and handsome as a hottentot prince, is still single, and, what is more, apparently insensible to all her provocations.

There has never been any gossip about him and women in Bantouville, where the private life of every higher-up is discussed daily by the black minority. As is the case with Adiami's own boss, Colonel Sar. Everyone knows that he lives almost connubially with a callipygous blonde toubabess who could be his daughter, but only as a figure of speech, since it would be hard to imagine that the genes of someone as totally African as he could be imperceptible to that extent in his posterity as of the first generation. It might be possible, but it wouldn't stand up to an anaylsis of properly conducted paraconjugal research.

"Here, drink this, commander," she says handing him a brimming glass.

The officer feels his heart skip a beat at being addressed thus, but he is anxious not to show his hand too soon, so he doesn't let it show. He will wait until the dessert to make his revelation, and then he will dispose of this label of commander which already sounds out of date to his ears.

"A toast to your successes, gazelle!" he says.

From the first swallows of the heady, artfully prepared mixture, Adiami knows he has been had. He feels full of physical ardor but completely without will. He has fallen for the old drink trick like a high school boy, and has reached the point of no return. So he may as well let things take their course. But although he cannot hope to escape the machinations of this succubus, he intends nevertheless, with what lucidity remains, to put up a struggle when the moment of truth arrives. As for Seynabou, imbued with all the primordial matriarchal power, she watches her prey with little ambiguous chuckles. Now she empties her glass without batting an eyelid and gestures toward the bar:

"So, Commander," she asks, "are we going to go off half-cocked?"

He forces himself to articulate: "You pour it, I'll drink it," although he is now merely putty in the hands of an expert vamp.

Suddenly he feels poorly. A tom-tom goes off in his forehead. He falls back into his chair, braces his neck against the back, rubs his eyes with an incredulous air. He knows he is facing the bar. Seynabou is at the bar, he knows that too, since the clinking of the glasses and the clank of the bottles strike his ears painfully. On the other hand, as if in a dream, he sees only a mist over there, at the heart of which a silhouette moves with disturbing slowness. Suddenly something like a burst of machine gun fire is hammering at his skull, penetrating it violently, drilling, drilling . . . .

The young woman shouts to him, "Telephone!"

Vaguely, he attempts to get up, then gives up with a wave of his hand.

"I'm not home!"

Seynabou returns, lively, bright, already victorious:

"That's sweet of you not to be home to anyone when you're with me."

Should he say something? He doesn't even have time to because Seynabou has handed him a glass which he empties mechanically, like medicine, with the result that the tom-toms go off in his head again. He must absolutely, and without further delay, get some solid food into his stomach, or he will not be able to answer for his health.

In a husky voice that was intended to be loud he says:

"Charles Henry, you may serve!"

Then throwing gallantry to the winds, he rushes to the table before the mixture can take over completely.

When did he eat? What did he eat? How?

When did he take off his uniform? These questions are destined to remain unanswered. He comes to upstairs, in his room, in his bed, with the fragrant Seynabou by his side. The subsequent action could be summed up in the form of a laconic communiqué on military operations (although in this case it is the civilian Seynabou who has the upper hand): after sustaining for an hour the pressure of our advanced salients, which are deployed in an enveloping movement, the enemy responded timidly with a volley of shots and then retreated in a rout.

The hostilities were at that point when, from the ground floor there arrives the sound of a loud storm of abuse. Adiami, sober by this time, listens and it is not long before he realizes what a wasp's nest he has gotten himself into. It is a furious Colonel Sar, upbraiding the unfortunate Charles Henry.

"What the hell is going on," thunders the colonel, "I've been calling for over an hour and nobody answers. What's the meaning of this!"

"Cuhcuh, curn, cur . . ." stutters Charles Henry.

"That's enough! Cur, yourself, batrachophage! Go tell your master he's got five minutes to get his ass in here or I'm coming to get him myself. Carry on!"

Shouted as it is, the colonel's threat has not escaped the notice of the bedroom's two occupants, and before the boy has even knocked at the door, Adiami is jumping out of bed, and without thinking, addresses his companion confidentially, pressing her with entreaties.

"Please don't make any noise, my gazelle! Get dressed and take the back stairs out of here. The colonel's as mean as a horned viper. If he saw you . . . ."

"Okay, okay, I'm splitting!" she says, offended, "What a day!"

"Good! I'm going down to see him. I'll call you this evening."

"What for? I've had enough laughs for one day, believe it or not!" she answers, sarcastic and aloof.

Hastily pulling on his house bubu, Adiami rushes towards the door and finds himself face to face with Charles Henry, hand up ready to knock.

"All right, I'm on my way! Go back down to your quarters!"

With that he hurtles down the stairs and comes out into the living room to face the colonel's fury. The latter is pacing nervously back and forth, his right hand behind his back, his gaze fixed on a watch which he holds in his left hand. Hearing him come in, Sar pivots with one movement. Adiami freezes and corrects his position which is a fairly grotesque one, dressed as he is in a red and black checked house dress.

The colonel explodes: "What the hell is going on, Adiami? What do you think this is, a circus?"

"Cuhcuh, cur . . . ." Adiami tries to articulate, still standing at attention.

"My word, it's an epidemic. Now you're stuttering, just like your houseboy! At ease! Go change, and hop it! You've got three minutes. Dismissed!

Adiami goes back up the stairs as fast as he came down, dashes into his room, where Seynabou's perfume still lingers, but fortunately she is already gone. The colonel's shouts covered the sound of the car taking off, he supposes, as he changes his clothes pensively.

Disaster! Right in the middle of the bed is the reporter's pink nylon panties. Despite the agitation, his first reaction is pride: in her precipitous retreat the enemy has abandoned an important piece of strategic material on the battlefield. But on second thought . . . That bitch! She did it on purpose. A woman doesn't forget something like that! Least of all, Seynabou, who is so careful, so calculating! Not a calimbé, the queen pin of feminine undergarments. No, she wanted to compromise him. What a scene there would have been if Colonel Sar had come up to the room!

If that's how it is, he'll teach this chick a thing or two! Without wasting an instant he opens a drawer, grabs a large-size official envelope with coat-of-arms and appropriate letterhead: *Republic of Baoulia, Ministry of Defense, Bomb Squad of the Federal Government of the O.B.E.* Then he folds the calimbé, slips it into the envelope which he licks with a prudent tongue-stroke, seals it, allows himself the pleasure of stamping it with the rubber stamp of the Main Office of the Bomb Squad, and rings for Charles Henry who, well-trained, appears instantly by the service stairs.

"Go take this letter to Miss Seynabou Banzawa at the Baoulian Press Agency, Rue des Flamboyants, down Souane's way.

"Yes, Commander."

"Wait, take this, too."

He attaches a calling card which reads, in engraved letters: *With Commander Adiami's compliments.*

"Deliver it to her in person, got that?" he adds.

3

The curious goings-on they have just witnessed leave the detectives very perplexed. These are the facts: the corporal-chauffeur has been expeditiously dismissed; the bad bitch with the convertible went gaily into the villa as if she owned the place almost two full hours ago; now Colonel Sar comes roaring up to the door, driving his own service car, and hurls himself into Adiami's house with a mean expression on his face, followed by a riot of violently slammed doors. It is all a mystery. Yet Baobab knows that these honorable servants of the State have seen a thing or two since they first began using up the public baouls with tails, surveillances and interrogations.

"What do you think?" asks the older man.

"Looks fishy."

"You won't be risking the white list with an answer like that, nigger! But the Boz won't pin a medal on you for it, either, believe me!"

Ever since the occasion, which almost ended in tragedy, of Edgar Dupont's interrogation, when Bozambo called him a fire-eater, the detective knows what it means to talk. Not that he fears his chief more or detests him less, far from it; but he would be very sorry if his young acolyte, for whom he considers himself morally responsible, were to be called on the carpet by the Inspector General, searching for a pretext to assert his professional standing and so to regain command of the situation.

"That is to say: for the moment we can draw no conclusions," says the novice, trying to be more precise. "We'll have to wait! If the colonel had shown up with his toubabess, it could have meant a foursome. But two to one . . . ."

"You know, you missed your calling, my man. You shouldn't have been a cop . . ."

"What should I have been?"

"A pimp. Mind you, it almost comes to the same thing."

The young man concedes a bull's eye. In his heart he knows he asked for it. So he avoids taking offense, especially since his colleague outranks him.

And now the young woman is shooting precipitously out of the service entrance and leaps into her sports model Derlin-Zinsou. They have barely time to exchange a questioning glance before she has started off, taking the corner like a bat out of hell with a screech of tires, followed by a raging roar of the engine, irresistibly pulled by its eighty zebupower.

"Hey, was it the colonel that put the fear of Baobab into her?"

"I guess so! Must have caught them in the sack!" answers the younger one, who is most certainly fixated.

The other, touched by the contagion, follows suit:

"She got her threads together damned fast. That's not a woman, that's a robot! Anyway, all this doesn't tell us what the old man came sniffing after."

"We'll have to wait!" the novice says again. "It always pays off, as my old boss in Baoul-Bled used to say."

"Who was your boss?"

"Doesn't matter; he's dead."

"Well, you can't say he waited very long. Don't believe everything your bosses tell you, son!"

And yet, the young one is right. Charles Henry appears at the service entrance with a large envelope in hand. Panting, cautious and nervous, his bubu clinging to his body, he hugs the wall and walks with long halting strides. Caught up in his mission he heads straight for the detectives without even seeing them. A leathery hand grabs him by the back of the neck, leaving him just the time to stifle a cry and to freeze.

"Not so fast, toubab! What's the hurry?"

"Let me go! I haven't done anything!"

"Who said you did?"

"Then why are you arresting me?"

"We're not arresting you, my boy. Just checking your I.D. We saw you come out of the commander's house and we want to find out why. Okay?"

When he hears this, Charles Henry makes his case worse by a stupid reflex action: he tries to hide the envelope in his bubu.

"Let's see that!" interjects the other cop.

And to make it quite clear that he isn't joking, he hits him viciously in the ribs with a mandingo-club, which has the reputation of knocking the wind out of you without leaving a mark. Under the impact of the blow, Charles Henry doubles up, and his face twists into a grimace. That is all it takes: he is neither brave nor foolhardy; and he lets the envelope fall into the nearest black hand.

The senior detective, who was on the spot to receive the offering, grabs it quickly, scans the various indications and lets out a long admiring whistle despite himself.

"Well, well! An official envelope! I see! Mister . . . uh, Mister, what is it? I've forgotten your name."

The boy falls into the trap and gives his name immediately.

"Charles Henry Durand."

"You're in luck, fried-potato-eater!" interrupts the younger detective. "If you'd said Dupont, you'd have gotten another kiss from Mandingo. When I hear bullshit, it makes my hand go off all by itself," he finishes, showing a fist the size of a ham.

"Let's get back to business!" the senior officer continues. "So, Mister Durand . . . That's Charles Henry for the ladies and his boss, isn't that right, my little man? So Mister Charles Henry Durand is involved in military communications?"

"The commander told me to take this to the Baoulian Press Agency."

"Don't waste your breath, boy! I can read! And here's what I read: addressee: nothing! On the other hand there is a visiting card *With Commander Adiami's compliments.* And it feels funny for a letter, wouldn't you say?" he persists, palpating the envelope carefully.

"Lemme see," says the other, taking it from him to feel it attentively. "Strange, this stationery! Wha' d'you think?"

"I think this isn't a good place to talk. There's a certain lack of intimacy."

"You're right, colleague. We'd be more comfortable at the Federal Building."

So they carry Charles Henry off. After the colonel's storm of abuse, here is the invitation to travel. For sure, this is not his lucky day.

Immediately informed of the interception of the servant, Bozambo takes the elevator down to the "confessional," situated in the basement, to direct the interrogation in person. The confiscated envelope is worth more by itself than the longest deposition so the client shouldn't have to be grilled too much. Bozambo takes the envelope into a corner and opens it.

"An oyster-piece in a package!" he marvels. "Holy Baobab, what can this mean?"

The detectives, who do not know the meaning of the word oyster-piece, although it appears in the Petit Dictionnaire Labrune, exchange doubtful glances. Convinced that it is a technical term from military jargon, they nevertheless prepare to punish the young toubab for having attempted to endanger the internal and external security of the State by stealing this highly confidential document. Bozambo did not let them see the contents of the envelope and now he comes back to Charles Henry who is sitting on a hard stool exposed, like someone in a photographer's studio, to the beams of powerful spotlights.

"Tell me, Durand, where did you steal this from?"

The Durand in question, firmly gripped by the shoulders by one of the cops, is blinking constantly under the glaring light and is hiccupping, on the verge of tears. By way of answer he grimaces painfully and says:

"Me? Steal it?"

"If you didn't steal it, then someone must have given it to you to deliver?"

Charles Henry says nothing but acquiesces with an imperceptible nod. In a flash Bozambo realizes that he has Adiami by the short hairs. An old local proverb has it that: *Every wild boar has his fatal Saturnal,* or to put it more clearly, sooner or later we must leave the pleasures of the sty for the road to the slaughterhouse. Adiami's hour has come and Bozambo will be trading the sacrificial victim's cowl for the executioner's bubu. He turns to his subordinates:

"Hey, you two! Go see if there's something in the files on this guy!"

"Yes, chief," obeys the senior one, somewhat disgruntled.

As soon as they have left, Bozambo moves toward the detained man and speaks to him gently:

"Listen, Charles Henry, now that we're alone why don't you tell me what happened."

"Alone? I'm not alone! With these spotlights . . . ."

"You're right," says Bozambo and turns them off. "You're very lucky, you know, to be interrogated by the Inspector General in person. You know, I'm absolutely against violence. And I'm sure you don't want to rot in jail, so if you tell me the truth, I'll have you released at once and all this will remain between us."

This speech has no effect on the toubab who is in a position to know that the promises of the police are never kept, especially when the police are from the mother country. So he limits himself to saying:

"I already told the truth: the commander gave me this envelope."

"You're wrong, Charles Henry! If you don't come up with something better than that before those two hulks come back, you'll have to deal with them. And then . . . ."

Bozambo has found the conclusive argument. His threat has awakened a dull intercostal pain in the boy, a tangible souvenir of the mandingo-clubbing he received on the sidewalk. Already in the open air, where they could have been seen, the hulks had no inhibitions about hitting him brutally. What would it be like here, on their turf, within these four walls! So Charles Henry comes clean, tells the whole story with plenty of details to add to those in the detective's report and manages without being aware of it, to give

Bozambo one of the most pleasurable moments of his life.

"You're quite sure it was Colonel Sar who beat them out of their bush?"

"Yes sir, Inspector General sir. They were up there when he arrived. He raised hell because no one answered the phone. But he didn't have time to see the lady."

"And you left the colonel down there?"

"Yes sir, Inspector General sir."

"Do you know what's in the envelope?"

"No sir, Inspector General sir."

"That's enough! You don't have to repeat Inspector General Sir every time!"

"All right, Inspector Gene. . . ."

"Good Baobab! Is your needle stuck, or what? So you're sure you don't know what's in the envelope?"

"I didn't have time to find out. I had to cut out in a hurry because of the colonel. In the street your two guys collared me . . . ."

"O.K. I believe you. If you don't have a record I'll release you with a little something for your trouble. But on one condition: I keep the envelope and you don't say anything to your boss. If he asks you, just say you ran your errand."

"That'll be difficult. He asked me to deliver it in person. If he ever calls the lady, I could lose my job!"

"Don't worry about that," answers Bozambo, "I'll take care of it."

Then he extracts three thousand-baoul bills from his pocket and hands them to Charles Henry who hurriedly closes his fingers over the Witch-Doctors without noticing that their eyes are out.

"Thank you Inspector General sir. Thank you, it's too much!"

"Don't overdo it! If you really think it's too much, get a basket of pomegranates for your boss when you go to the market. Tell him it's from his friend Bozambo!"

The door opens. The senior detective has returned, followed, as always, by his young associate.

"Chief, there's nothing in the files on him."

"Very good! He can go. Go on, get out!" orders Bozambo to Charles Henry, who leaps from his stool and vanishes into the hall.

"The case is closed," continues Bozambo for the detectives' benefit. "Cease all surveillance of the subject Adiami!"

"But chief . . . ."

Bozambo interrupts him: "That little Charles Henry is one of my informers. You wouldn't have guessed, would you?"

4

Face to face with Adiami, who is very ill at ease, in spite of having put on his uniform again, Colonel Sar is as jumpy as a hippo on a hot tin roof. Needless to say, if he persisted in trying to phone, and then deemed it necessary to go in person, he must have a good reason. Adiami knows this and is dying to know why, but he also knows that first he will have to put up with some more blustering from his chief, who is a past master in the art of making people uncomfortable.

"Adiami, what the hell were you up to that was so important you didn't hear the phone?"

"I didn't know it was you, Colonel."

"You're avoiding the question, my boy!" observes the colonel, suddenly starting to sniff like a Kabyle shepherd at a dead set.

Given his trained sense of smell, and Seynabou's excesses in the matter of perfume, it is a miracle that the old soldier hadn't smelled the truth sooner. It is true that he was so enraged upon his arrival, that he shouted and stormed so much, that his sense of smell was temporarily out of commission. But now he is calmer, and unless he has a bad cold, which doesn't seem to be the case, it shouldn't be long before he reacts to the tenacious fragrance which lingers in the air; the same perfume that he inhales voluptuously every evening on his young Bantouvillian mistress' neck. Now he is wrinkling his forehead, turning his head from side to side, stretching his neck and sniffing harder than ever:

"Adiami, there's a strong smell of *Zambeze Flower* here! Don't deny it, I know perfectly well what I'm talking about!"

This allusion strikes Adiami like a slap in the

face. Disconcerted, he cannot help but relive, momentarily, his recent paltry military spending. The colonel's brutal burst of laughter pours salt onto the wound.

"A sharp-shooter, eh?" he snickers, "pounding like a son of a bitch, my boy, eh? No wonder you didn't hear the 'phone! Goddamn, couldn't you wait until nighttime, like everybody else, you ravisher? Be careful! You don't live to be old with that kind of work-out . . . A married woman, hmm?"

Adiami is on the rack and wonders if that animal, Charles Henry, was able to revenge him by delivering the envelope in person. Maybe no doubt he wasn't able to rise to the situation—it's easier to have your mouth open than your hand out, as far as that goes—but if the journalist should ever be inclined to fool around in the future, he can always offer his own version of the story with a certain pungency of its own: Seynabou, frightened by his treatment of her, had no choice but to run like a rat, without waiting for her calimbé.

"Okay," the colonel continues, "I don't want to make a thing of it. I'm even willing to forget this whole matter. My calls must have put you in a hell of a spot: it's never a good idea to interrupt one communication for another. Anyway, let's close this parenthesis, if you will permit me the metaphor!"

"Thank you, Colonel!"

"Here's what I came for. A little more than an hour ago, a coded telex arrived from Baoul-Bled. This is a serious moment, Adiami, The Baoulian government, following a proposal of President Mango Zekodene, (who, as you know, has set himself the task of decolonizing Europe) has decided to grant the Gauls internal autonomy."

"But that's madness, Colonel! They aren't ripe for it!"

"Calm down, my young friend! The role of the military man is to obey. Furthermore, you should know that the president retains full powers for six months. And he consulted the constitutional council which gave a favorable opinion on his proposal."

Adiami is becoming indignant: "But Colonel, the O.B.E. is Baoulia! We've been here for two centuries. We have our monuments here, our culture, our dead!"

The colonel answers serenely: "Let me finish. The debates will come later. So, always according to the telex, the president will announce the event to the people in a big speech over radio and television in a few days. There will most certainly be an extraordinary commotion in Bantouville, probably disturbances, a renewed outbreak of activity by the nationalist movements, who knows? In any case that's where we come in. We have to set up, as of now, security arrangements, discreetly grid the city in such a way as to be able to contain any demonstrations."

"We could just send all suspects to join Escartefigue in jail! That's the best solution!"

"You're wrong, Adiami! I can tell you right now that, on the contrary, there will be a whole slew of presidential amnesties. All political prisoners, or almost all, anyway, will be released soon. You have to be realistic, my young friend, and not make the same mistakes as the Maghrebins. Look at the problems they're having in Corsica, that bloody and futile struggle to which they've been reduced! They're on trial before the whole world. Their regime is threatened from the inside: the nation is rumbling, the economy is crumbling, the army is grumbling. And in spite of all of Moktar Alas' authority, they're on the verge of civil war."

This old murky and murderous Corsican matter has been growing for the last five years like a gangrene that could spread at any moment. The Maghrebin Republic, just recovering from an abortive pacification mission, in the course of which Scandinavia regained her independence, was obliged to send an expeditionary force into the Mediterranean. The island patriots, not satisfied with waging a subversive war in their native mountains, brought unrest even into the mother country with bombings and arson in industrial installations.

This couldn't go on. The Maghrebin people demanded something new and reasonable. That was an ambiguous, elastic request. It was believed that by that they meant a rapid quelling of the rebellion, whereas what they hoped for most was peace at last, a reduction of red tape, an effective campaign against the high cost of living and the return of their young men from the army, so that they too might participate in the economic expansion of the country.

The Maghrebin Democratic Front, which had been brought to power by a wave of popularity, was a kind of bicephalous political monster, and thus condemned from birth. It designated the populist Amor Ben Zitoun as head of government. Ben Zitoun, who had allegedly analysed the deep-rooted causes of the Corsican crisis and invented a solution, made (according to him) a revolutionary decision, immediately following his investiture. He would go in person to swear in a resident minister at Ahmedville, the island's capital.

In reality, this was no innovation. His colleague and beloved enemy, El Hadj Slimane, the other head of the Maghrebin Democratic Front, had, not so long before, pulled a similar coup with respect to the Sicilian rebellion. Head of the government at that time, he had suddenly gone to Palermo, bearing an offer of internal autonomy. But he was careful not to go out of the residential palace, or to face the activist Maghrebin minority: everything happened with dispatch, in the greatest privacy, without fanfares or brass bands.

As for Ben Zitoun, he was euphoric from his recent electoral success and convinced of his legitimacy. He wanted to do it all out in the open.

So now we find him in Ahmedville, with the resident minister by his side. He thought he could quiet the crowd, which was teeming with White Feet, by appealing to their patriotism. Weren't they shouting "Maghrebin Corsica"? No sooner had he arrived at the Monument to the Dead, a magnificent bouquet in the national colors in his arms, than a half dozen rotten tomatoes and soft-boiled eggs rained on him, spoiling his nice Solal fez. Electrified by these considerations, his white jeba all runny and sticky, Ben Zitoun has just understood. "Maghrebin Corsica," he shouted. And that same evening, after this sudden conversion, he retraced his steps back to the mother country with his superfluous minister. The forty-fourth Republic has just received a fatal blow. Nobody knows it yet, except perhaps the great heroic and respected Moktar Alas, who lives a retiring life in his native douar at Colibri-les-deux-Mosquées. Self-sacrifice and love of country will bring him out of his retreat to accept the poisoned gift of the presidency and to announce to the Corsicans that he has understood them.

Baoulia cannot expect to be so fortunate, since she has no such providential men in reserve. President Mango Zekodene, as far as that goes, has always been a liberal partisan of the gradual emancipation of colonized peoples. The time has come to act, and to profit from the Maghrebin experience. This is what Colonel Sar is trying to make this subordinate understand. But Adiami is unreclaimable, definitively undermined by the virus of imperialsim and he protests:

"The Gauls in power? I will never be an accomplice to such dereliction of responsibility!"

"In that case, you have no choice but to request recall to Baoulia, my boy! I'll sign it without reservation. But as for your promotion to lieutenant-colonel, you can kiss that good-bye!"

"What? You knew, Colonel?"

"I've known for a long time! And in spite of our differences of opinion, I've done nothing to intefere with your career. The report which I was asked to do on you and which I sent to the Ministry of Defense would prove that to you."

Adiami doesn't know what to say, and the ring of the telephone gets him out of a difficult situation. He would never have expected such objectivity from the colonel; had the roles been reversed he would have persecuted any subordinate as recalcitrant as he had been until now. He goes to pick up the receiver, but Sar beats him to it.

"Let me answer it! I warn you that if it's that woman, wanting to do a follow-up, I have news for her . . . Hello!" he snaps, "Who's there . . . . Well, well, yes, yes, quite right. Come and join us! We can kick the situation around . . . Right! See you later . . ."

"That was Bozambo," he says, hanging up the phone. "He's coming here."

"Here? What does he want?" Adiami is disturbed.

"He got a telex too. The army and the police are to work together to plan the security measures for the moment when they make the announcement of internal autonomy. Also, Bozambo says he has to see you right away. So if he comes here he can kill two birds with one stone."

"See me? Why?"

"We'll find out soon enough!"

5

The civilities were hastily concluded between Bozambo, as aloof as a cavolin* in front of a shoe, and Adiami, anxious and wary. From the expression on the face of the great chief of Territorial security, it is clear that he isn't here for fun and games. From the moment Charles Henry told him of the colonel's unexpected arrival and annoyance, he had worked out his plan: to launch a wide-scale surprise attack and put his adversary in the position of improvising his defense in the presence of an unimpeachable witness. Dressed in a dark bubu, the lapel of which bears the rosette of the Immortal Baobab, he is gravely going through a voluminous file which lies on the table before him.

"Where shall we begin?" asks Sar, to break the ice.

"Very simple!" answers Bozambo laconically, "There are two aspects to the security problem:

*Bare-footed hermit

the current situation, and that which will result from the official announcement of internal autonomy."

This purely technical approach to the present set of circumstances reassures Adiami slightly and he persuades himself that no personal considerations will crop up during the discussion. That thought is enough to loosen the knot which has been racking the pit of his stomach since Bozambo's call.

"Sensible!" he approves, anxious to prove his existence.

"That's better! . . . Shall I begin?" continues Bozambo, with a glance toward his old friend Sar, who acquiesces with a nod.

So far, so good, thinks Adiami. For sure the colonel must still be furious about the incident with the phone and from his subordinate's insubordination, but he's an honorable man, so the chances are slight that he'll go out of his way to stomp me. As for Bozambo, he's caught up in the requirements of general security and seems to have forgotten anything else. The word of the hour is take it easy.

"A refreshment?" proposes Adiami, more and more at ease. Bozambo returns the serve:

"In theory, never on duty. But today I'll make an exception."

"Palm wine? Tafia rum from the coast? . . ."

"Is there any pomegranate juice?"

Adiami is startled and a hunted look comes over his face.

"Alas! No."

"Too bad! It would have made an excellent opening," hints Bozambo.

"Opening?"

"Yes, but let's get back to the matter at hand. . . . So, at the present time, Bantouville is relatively calm. The principal explanation seems to be the beginning of wintering. Traditionally, in fact, there is a lull in subversive activities with the return of the cold weather. This year, for example, the statistics I have are particularly significant: from one hundred seventeen arrests or summonses daily during summering, the average has dropped to thirteen, although these last are almost entirely common law crimes. Obviously, this lull does not preclude disturbances tomorrow. The Archduke and his partisans are perhaps preparing some spectacular coup. Nevertheless my staff has the situation well in hand. And if it hadn't been for this recent Dupont affair. . . ."

"Ah, yes, the Dupont affair," the colonel murmurs evasively.

"Come on, Sar! The suitcase abandoned by a fugitive, in which the infantrymen found a package addressed to Edgar Dupont, extension of Rue Birago. . . . Do you remember, Commander?"

Astonished, Adiami asks: "Aren't we getting a little formal?"

"Why not? Do you remember or do I have to refresh your memory? The matter originated in your office, if I'm not mistaken. On the sixteenth of Bananuary, to be precise," specifies Bozambo in a neutral tone, still referring to his file.

"That's right!" agrees Adiami. That pile of papers is making him nervous.

"Tell us, Commander!"

Bozambo's express desire for pomegranate juice, though seemingly innocuous, was the first thrust. It was totally unexpected and threw Adiami off guard. Although the attacker then desisted from pursuing his advantage, the respite was merely a refinement. Adiami has his back to the wall again, charged with explaining himself. He must muster all his caution in order to sum up the Dupont affair without leaving his adversary an opening, because now he knows: the match has begun. Bozambo is marking him down, waiting for an advantageous opening.

"Well, some time ago, one of our patrols chased a native who managed to escape but jettisoned a suitcase which contained a suspicious-looking package."

"What was in the package?" interrupts Bozambo.

"Some pomegranates."

"What kind?"

"I don't understand," confesses Adiami hypocritically.

But it takes more than that to discourage Bozambo who has just set in motion an irrevocable machine. The psychological moment is his at last: Adiami is cornered and Sar is more and more perplexed. This is the moment to lay his cards on the table, to sow confusion and prove that he is the master of the situation.

"No matter," he continues in a curt voice, extracting a sheet of notebook paper from the file on the table. "I'll tell you. . . . "*My dear Edgar, the grape harvest has not been too bad. . . .* Shall I go on?"

"What's this all about?" demands the colonel.

Sar's astonishment takes Bozambo by surprise. He had been sure that the letter was a gift from the colonel, although the absence of a stamp. . . .

Maybe it's better this way, he thinks. The important thing is that I have it. And that my organization gets the credit.

"What it's about is obvious. The commander wanted to ridicule the chief of Federal Security by making up a story of explosives! But, as it happens, I am neither blind, nor one-eyed like the thousand-baoul bills that he amuses himself by passing me on the Q.T., by the bundle, taking advantage of my trust in him. There were never any explosives in the package for Dupont: the pomegranates came straight from the family orchard."

"Goddammit! Adiami, say something! Do you realize what's happening?" the colonel urges, and in him, in this precise instant, the entire Baoulian Army is shamed.

Completely crushed, Adiami says nothing and Sar's humiliation is total. But Bozambo takes up the offensive again:

"So we have proved that there never were any explosives in the suitcase. Any more than there was correspondence in the official envelope I have here, which is stamped moreover, with your department's letterhead, my dear Sar, and accompanied by a thank-you note from Commander Adiami. . . ."

"Where did you get that letter? That is mail theft!" cries an indignant Adiami.

"And exchanging good five-thousand baoul bills for worthless thousand-notes, isn't that theft? But never mind. You claim it's correspondence. What kind of document is it?"

"You have no right!"

"Wrong! I have every right to stop a native who leaves a Baoulian officer's house precipitously by the back door, hiding an official envelope in his bubu. I'll admit I was more concerned than the matter warranted, it's true. For once the person was neither a spy nor a thief. . . . But I wasn't convinced of that until later, at the Federal Building when I examined the contents of the envelope, if I may specify that once again. . . ."

"Let me see that!" interrupts the colonel.

"Do you really want to see it?" asks Bozambo.

"What do you mean, do I want to see it!" cries Sar. "Who's in charge here! Come on, give it to me, Boz."

Bozambo gives him the entire file forthwith; the colonel pounces on the envelope, thrusts in his hand and pulls out Seynabou's pink nylon panties.

His face twists suddenly and he throws the object on the table as if it were radioactive. He is motionless, the whites of his eyes are whiter than ever, open to the maximum, his eyebrows nearly touch his hairline; fists clenched, he leaps to his full height and, foaming at the mouth, he thunders at Adiami:

"Are you trying to make a fool of the Republic, Commander? A woman's calimbé in an official envelope! That's the last straw! You'll pay for that, my boy! All these items will be attached to the report I'm sending today to Baoul-Bled on your obsessive behaviour: imaginary grenades, which have Federal Security working overtime; willful profanation of paper-money (surely you can't be unaware of the repressive measures which have been decided in high places to punish this heinous crime); now you turn our official envelopes into bags for dirty laundry and distribute them throughout the city! And you dare to pontificate, to dispute our president's humanitarian actions, to give lessons on political morality to an administration which pays you to see that our flag is respected, while you spend your time desecrating it and screwing at inappropriate hours!

What you need is a psychiatrist, Adiami! You have what our early pioneers used to suffer from, blood on the brain!"

As he hears this, the most insane ideas jostle each other in Adiami's head. All is lost now, including his fifth plumed stripe. How much shame all in one day! To take Bozambo's riposte without a fight, to lose the colonel's esteem and the army's confidence forever (it's obvious that with so many crushing pieces of evidence, Sar's report will be terribly effective). What is there left for him besides recall to Baoulia and summary punishment to boot? The whole affair will be bruited about, commented upon in the governmental circles of Baoul-Bled. "That curious soldier, who is he? . . . You don't know? He's a former commander of the colonial troops. He lost his marbles completely in Bantouville, blood on the brain! Seems he saw explosives everywhere, put out the Witch-Doctor's eyes, and composed his correspondence on a strange kind of letter paper: women's pink nylon calimbés!" And then it will be all over for him, because even the minister who is so afraid of him will now have a weapon and will accept no more blackmail! Well, if all is lost he might as well get it over with! But how? True, there's his service pistol whose grip gleams close by in the holster hanging on a peg. What an extraordinary picture it would present: the suicide of a dishonored officer before the very eyes of a colonel and a director of Federal

Security, both on duty! What posthumous rehabilitation of his good name! But also what blood, what an affecting spectacle: the body of a thirty-year-old athlete lying at their feet in a necessarily indecent posture, disfigured, emptying itself in torrents through a hideous cranial wound all mixed in with cerebral material and twitching grotesquely. Feh! Adiami is revolted and unconsciously mimics his protector the minister:

"Colonel, if it's my suicide you want, you can have it!"

"Spare me the melodrama!" shouts Sar, "Cash for smashed calabash! However, I'll say you're mentally deficient, so you'll be repatriated for medical reasons. That's the best I can do."

"Repatriated for medical reasons?"

"Yessir, that's what I said. Blood on the brain. You're not the first Baoulian to be struck by that scourge. Oh, great Keskonfé-Dessu, where are you now?"

"Never, do you hear me? Never!" protests Adiami.

Then turning to Bozambo.

"Sir, I demand satisfaction! With cavalry assegais! I'll send my seconds tomorrow!"

Bozambo, who has never been more sure of himself, snickers, and teases him.

"And who would your seconds be? Your boy, Charles Henry, and that reporter from Baoulia-Press?"

Undone by this last blow, Adiami sits, on the brink of madness.

"Let's cut out, Boz," proposes Sar. "We can discuss important things elsewhere. What have we to do with this nut?"

Epilogue

Bantouville is living joyful moments. The radio and television message of President Mango Zekodene has triggered a delirious enthusiasm. For eight days now, reflecting what is going on all over the O.B.E., the federal capital has been improvising hymns in honor of the great decolonizer, and dancing on every street corner to the rhythms of the java. In the streets gaudy bubus printed with the presidential portrait have appeared as if by magic on the Bantouvillians. Designed by expert couturiers, the printed motif decorates the derrieres of the wiggling natives so that, at every swivel, the President's face, thus prominently placed, expands and wrinkles, between a snicker and a sob. In the town halls, the civil servant's job is more monotonous than ever because each new father, temporarily abandoning the toubab calendar, proposes to baobaben his son Mango or his daughter Manga. Even the most nationalist ones, now convinced that the dark misery which has been strangling the people is about to end, go with the tide and make up compound names, like Mango-Leopold or Manga-Suzanne. Thus, the name of the illustrious Zekodene, imposed upon their posterity by the grateful will of the little people, will go down in history.

The one false note in this chorus of praise is the Pale Hand, who are used to working the honkies. Most of them are upset at having to give up the numerous material advantages conferred upon them by the colonial life: plentiful, docile and inexpensive servants; astronomical salaries, paid in C.B.E. baouls, plus the hardship allowance that is customary in the colonial world; administrative positions well beyond their capabilities, while in Baoulia they could not hope for the equivalent jobs; annual holidays in the mother country, often extended upon presentation of a signed note from a compliant doctor. For these, the privileged, autonomy is a real disaster.

Another category of discontented people are the boys, the fatous and the whole body of small toubab tradespeople, who are indifferent to political matters and who live off the African minority; for them the departure of the Pale Hand could cause a serious recession.

Most of the political prisoners have been released. A certain Georges-Edouard-Ferdinand Escartefigue was brought out of his cell and flown by private jet to Baoul-Bled, officially invited by Mango Zekodene to discuss the formation of the first autonomous government of the O.B.E., of which he is to assume the vice-presidency.

Various rumors are circulating about the possible make-up of the ministerial team. But the only reliable information comes from the Archduke, who knows perfectly well that he will be named Minister of Public Works, Transportation and Housing; that Edgar Dupont, who has given consistent proof of his competence in the field, will be made Minister of Welfare and Population. As for Anatole Dupont, who does not know it as yet, His Excellency Prosper Yoplaboume is seriously considering appointing him his Chief of Staff. It is a characteristic of the process of decolonization that it be accompanied by abrupt changes on the individual level: one activist leaves the chamois and pail of soapy water for a brand new minister's portfolio; another his welfare card for a ministerial pass.

Since, according to the framework law, the ministers of National Defense and of the Interior, among others, will remain under the jurisdiction of the mother country, Colonel Sar and Inspector General Bozambo are preparing to reorient themselves toward a new career side by side with Escartefigue and the Archduke. A little while ago, they wished Commander Adiami bon voyage. This is a euphemism: at the time of his embarcation from the gate at Duke Ellington airport, he was wearing a strait jacket.

Key to Certain Terms (first appearance)

English Edition	French Edition	
p. 1	p. 11	***Sékouane: la Seine*** (from the Latin Sequana).
p. 1	p. 11	***Saramakaye:*** an allusion to the Guyanese ethnic group the "Saramakas" who are of african origin and who reconstructed their civilization in the forests of French Guyana after escaping from slavery.
p. 1	p. 11	***Abou-Zouzouf,*** père de la théorie de l'absoluité: an allusion to Albert Einstein (opposition between relativity and "absolutivity").
p. 1	p. 12	***la tour Abdoulaye:*** la tour Eiffel.
p. 1	p. 12	***la butte Mozamba:*** Montmartre.
p. 5	p. 15	***Amadou-Koumba:*** *Les Contes d'Amadou Koumba.*
p. 6	p. 16	***la main blême:*** allusion to the "Main Rouge", a French activist organization of North Africa before the independence of the Maghreb countries.

p. 6	p. 16	***Gueules roses:*** reference to a Chester Himes character (Pink Toes?).
p. 6	p. 17	***Baoul-Bled:*** a near anagram of Bab-El-Oued, which was a section of Algiers which was a center for French activists during the war for Algerian independence. The city which is supposed to represent Baoul-Bled is Abidjan.
p. 8	p. 18	***Champs-Baobabs:*** Champs-Elysées.
p. 8	p. 18	***La Rue Birago:*** Birago Diop author of *Les Contes d'Amadou Koumba.*
p. 8	p. 18	***L'avenue Modibo:*** Modibo Keita, former President of Mali.
p. 8	p. 19	***Place des Hosties-Noires:*** poem by Senghor ("Hosties-Noires").
p. 8	p. 19	***Le boulevard Sékou:*** Sékou Touré.
p. 9	p. 20	***pieds valvanisés:*** allusion to a well-known French comic strip, "Les Pieds Nickelés."
p. 9	p. 20	***Bobo Fikokin:*** allusion to the comic strip character, "Bibi Fricotin".

p. 10 p. 21 ***De Tamanrasset à Bastia:*** *De Dunkerque á Tamanrasset,* a slogan of the OAS in France during the Algerian war (1954-1962).

p. 12 p. 24 ***Bora Belkoukoune: BB,*** Brigitte Bardot.

p. 13 p. 24 ***Ouolové:*** the reversed spelling of the term *evolué* (evolved), used by the French to designate Africans who have received (and accepted) a European education, hence, are (or have) evolved into more than their original "savagery."

p. 13 p. 24 ***Zartan:*** Tarzan.

p. 15 p. 26 ***Mango Zékodène:*** a creole expression designating a variety of mango which is about the size of a turkey egg.

p. 17 p. 28 ***Côte d'Opale:*** Côte d'Azure.

p. 22 p. 33 ***La Place Léon-G.-Soumaké:*** Léon-Gontran Damas, great Guyanese poet.

p. 25 p. 37 ***Baoulie-Soir:*** the newspaper *France-Soir.*

p. 26	p. 38	***Koumba Couli-Cagou:*** Harriet Beecher Stowe.
p. 26	p. 38	***La Turne de l'Oncle Jules:*** *Uncle Tom's Cabin.*
p. 26	p. 38	***Vivi Oumarou:*** Victor Schoelcher, a French politician who advocated the abolition of slavery in the French colonies.
p. 27	p. 38	***Laclôture:*** Toussaint L'Ouverture.
p. 31	p. 43	***Tonton-Makoute:*** Haitian paramilitary terrorists.
p. 33	p. 46	***Le Lycée Behanzin-le-Grand:*** le Lycée Louis-le-Grand.
p. 38	p. 50	***D'Eugolles:*** Général de Gaulle.
p. 43	p. 55	***Bobo-Dioulasso:*** capital of the Republic of Upper Volta before the European partitioning of Africa by the Treaty of Berlin (1885).
p. 43	p. 55	***Kolombou:*** Columbus.
p. 47	p. 59	***Lamine Zamba:*** Aimé Césaire, leading writer (poet, playwright) and politician from Martinique.
p. 54	p. 65	***Patrice La Rumba:*** Patrice Lamumba.

p. 54 p. 65 ***Doudou Glissant:*** Edouard Glissant, leading writer from French Antilles.

p. 55 p. 66 ***Tintin-K.-Taillé:*** Justin Catayée, Deputé from French Guyane, a friend of the author, and very partial to smoking a pipe. He died in 1962.

p. 56 p. 67 ***Amokonte-Deumo:*** allusion to a phrase in *Le Cid* by Corneille: "A moi Comte, deux mots! "

p. 56 p. 67 ***Keskonfé-Dessu:*** Dessu is a Congolese name. Keskonfé is a phonetic transcription of Qu'est-ce qu'on fait, which means what are you doing? Or, "Qu'est-ce qu'on fait dessous" might be translated as "What is being done undercover."

p. 78 p. 91 ***Alioune-l'Insaisissable:*** Alioune Diop, director of the publishing house Présence Africaine.

p. 91 p. 105 ***L'Univers:*** the French newspaper, *Le Monde.*

p. 91 p. 105 ***Le Raseur:*** the French newspaper *Le Figaro* (Figaro of course referring to the Barber of Seville, consequently, the razor [raseur]).

p. 91	p. 105	***Le Crépuscule:*** French newspaper, *L'Aurore.*
p. 91	p. 105	***Témoignage Baobabiste:*** *Témoignage Chrétien,* a weekly French newspaper (progressive).
p. 92	p. 106	***Moktar Hélas:*** refers to De Gaulle because of a celebrated speech he made denouncing the terrorism of the OAS, saying, "Hélas, hélas, hélas! ".
p. 93	p. 107	***Toucan déplumé:*** the satirical French newspaper, *Le Canard Enchaîné.*
p. 132	p. 146	***Baoulie-Presse:*** French newspaper, *France-Presse.*
p. 134	p. 148	***zébus-vapeur:*** cheval-vapeur (horse power).
p. 137	p. 152	***Dictionnaire Labrune:*** the Larousse dictionary.
p. 147	p. 162	***Colibri-les-deux Mosquées:*** Colombes-les-deux Eglises, De Gaulle's family residence.